The Keepers

Donna Augustine

The Keepers

ISBN: 0615801951
ISBN-13: 978-0615801957

DEDICATION

To Jess, my muse.

A special thank you to Dragonfly Editing.

CONTENTS

	Dedication	iii
1	Chapter One	Pg 1
2	Chapter Two	Pg 9
3	Chapter Three	Pg 21
4	Chapter Four	Pg 31
5	Chapter Five	Pg 49
6	Chapter Six	Pg 59
7	Chapter Seven	Pg 68
8	Chapter Eight	Pg 74
9	Chapter Nine	Pg 82
10	Chapter Ten	Pg 111
11	Chapter Eleven	Pg 117
12	Chapter Twelve	Pg 125
13	Chapter Thirteen	Pg 137
14	Chapter Fourteen	Pg 141
15	Chapter Fifteen	Pg 150
16	Chapter Sixteen	Pg 164

17	Chapter Seventeen	Pg 175
18	Chapter Eighteen	Pg 182
19	Chapter Nineteen	Pg 187
20	Chapter Twenty	Pg 198
21	Chapter Twenty-One	Pg 210
22	Chapter Twenty-Two	Pg 221
23	Chapter Twenty-Three	Pg 229
24	Chapter Twenty-Four	Pg 234
25	Chapter Twenty-Five	Pg 240
26	Chapter Twenty-Six	Pg 251
27	Chapter Twenty-Seven	Pg 258
28	Chapter Twenty-Eight	Pg 277

Chapter One

"No, I can't wait until tomorrow. You need to take her tonight." I heard Maxine's voice in the kitchen. I'd been living with her and Charlie for the last two months, and as far as foster homes went, it was one of the better ones. Charlie would watch Sesame Street with me in the morning, and Maxine baked cookies sometimes. She had even made me a cake for my seventh birthday.

They lived in an apartment, but there was a park across the street that had a swing set. As far as homes go, it was the best I'd ever had, but now it was over.

"I won't have her here another night. There is something wrong with her," Maxine continued. She spoke in a strange breathy tone that I'd never heard her use before.

I peeked around the corner, keeping myself in the shadows of my still dark room. Maxine and Charlie were standing in the kitchen together. Charlie held one of Maxine's hands as her other

1

hand held the phone in a white knuckled grip. I'd just read that phrase in a book the other day and been looking for a fitting situation to use it. This seemed to be perfect. Only problem was, there was no one to say it to.

"Tell them," Charlie urged Maxine. Charlie was the one I usually liked to try out my flavorful verses on. He called me a savant the other day and smiled. I knew whatever it had meant had made him happy, but now he seemed to want me gone, too.

Maxine covered the phone piece and then replied to him, "I can't tell them everything. They'll think we're nuts. How are we going to ever get a child then?"

It was nice while it lasted. I had liked them.

"Fine, but if you're not here by tomorrow morning, I'm bringing her to you." I watched Maxine hang the phone back on its cradle on the mustard yellow kitchen wall.

"Thank god, they're coming. This kid is freaking me out," Charlie said, and then hugged Maxine. "I'm sorry, I know you thought maybe she was the one. There are lots of other kids."

I knew what they meant. They wanted a normal kid, not me. I pulled my worn green suitcase out of the closet and grabbed Henry, my stuffed penguin off the bed. "It's okay Henry, we don't need them. We don't need anyone."

2

Fifteen Years Later

The knocking at the door awakened me. Squinting one eye, not having the energy to open both yet, I looked at my alarm clock. One of the minute lights had burned out, so I had to round to the nearest ten minutes. Who in their right mind would be banging on my door at ten to six in the morning? I groaned because I knew the answer already. It was Mrs. Harvey; no one would ever accuse her of being in her right mind.

"Hang on!" I yelled toward the general vicinity of the door and started looking for pants. Even though I was sure it was Mrs. Harvey, answering the door in a t-shirt and underwear didn't seem like a good idea. Leaning down, I groped along the cluttered floor in the dark trying to find a pair of sweat pants. I kept forgetting to buy light bulbs, so I had rotated the bedroom light bulb to the living room light, where I liked to do all my studying. After accidentally stepping on one of my text books and stabbing myself with a pen, my hand finally landed on familiar cotton.

The knocking started up again and it felt as if my whole wall shook with the force of the old woman's pounding. "I'm coming," I said, as I made my way to the door of my small rented trailer.

3

Swinging the door open, before she could lay her little fists to the paint chipped surface again, I greeted my neighbor.

Mrs. Harvey was of an unknown age somewhere between eighty and a hundred, if I had to guess. She was very fond of baby blue eye shadow and bright red lipstick. She also liked to wear her hair in a bouffant. She owned the next trailer over with her husband, which looked like the Royal Palace compared to mine.

"Mrs. Harvey, what's wrong?"

"Josephine, Mr. Harvey's hip is still bothering him, can you come by later today?"

"Mrs. Harvey, I told you, I'm a premed student, not a doctor. I don't know how to do any of that stuff, yet."

"Can you come by later, anyway? It makes Mr. Harvey feel better."

Her sweet voice and the pleading look in her eyes were hard to turn down.

"Okay, sure, I've got the breakfast shift at the diner, and classes after that, but I should be able to swing by around seven?"

"I'll make you a nice dinner."

"That sounds good," I said, and I wasn't lying either. It sounded great. Mrs. Harvey was one of the best cooks I'd ever met. I knew that this wasn't so much about Mr. Harvey's hip, as much as that I reminded them of their daughter who had died many years ago.

After she left, I plopped down on my bed again. I lay there for about ten minutes before I looked at the clock, and I debated how many hours of sleep I could get. Problem was I hadn't been able to fall asleep last night until I had lain there for two hours. I didn't think my prospects were much better now.

I gave up and took a quick shower, instead, then grabbed the cleanest work clothes I could find and my chemistry book. I headed toward the bus stop three blocks away, figuring I could get the morning cook to give me a free omelet for breakfast while I studied before my shift.

Hours later, when I was sitting in my final lab class for the day, I felt like I was dead on my feet. My lab partner, Lacey, stood next to me. She was the one person I knew whom I considered almost a friend. Not because I saw her outside of school, because I didn't see anyone outside of school, I didn't see anyone outside of work, either, for that matter. I wasn't your typical twenty-something year old. When people realized I was a freak of nature, they usually didn't stick around for long. And when they couldn't run, they found a way to push me out. I'd learned that over and over again as a child, being shuttled from one foster home to the next. Every now and then I'd become friendly with someone like Lacey, or the Harvey's, but I

5

always knew somewhere deep inside it wouldn't last.

When I was a child, I used to think that every new home would be the one. My case counselor told me that it was just a matter of finding the right fit. I still remembered the day when I realized that this time wasn't going to be any different. The day I'd lost hope.

I had been six and living with one family for five months, an all time record, when the counselor picked me up at school. She had a list of excuses why they hadn't wanted me, but I knew she lied. I always knew a lie when I heard one. That wasn't why I was a freak. It's not some sort of gift, I think I'm just perceptive, and people always give a tell. That's what they call it in poker when people give up their hand. A tell.

"Jo!" Lacey was hitting me in the side. "I'm not doing this shit all by myself!"

Lacey's voice jolted me out of my half sleep just in time to see my pen floating in front of my face. I grabbed it and shoved it in my pocket before anyone else noticed.

"What?" I asked, now fully awake.

"You aren't helping." Lacey never lied. She might be a little hard on the senses sometimes, but she was painfully honest.

"Sorry, I'm just beat. I had the breakfast shift."

"Why don't you let me get you in with me at

Lacard? My uncle got promoted to pit boss. I'm positive he can get you in as a cocktail waitress. He already got me in and is going to get me some shifts in the high rollers pit. I bet he could get you in too."

The Lacard was the newest and most expensive casino on the Vegas Strip. When I did have free time, which was almost never, I liked to stroll through their high-end mall and imagine all the things I'd buy when I was a doctor one day.

"You wouldn't have to work as much then," Lacey added.

"I don't want…"

"Don't even start! I know! You hate favors. You can do it for me then, because when you work the morning shifts, you're barely human, and I find it to be a hostile work environment." Lacey had started prelaw before she switched to premed. According to her, she would've been a brilliant lawyer, but she decided her genius was better spent curing cancer.

I sat back and looked at her big pleading brown eyes. They were strikingly dark compared to her bleached blond hair, a combination that might have been harsh on someone else but somehow worked well for her.

I'd had classes on and off with Lacey for the last two years. She had gotten to know me pretty well, or as well as anyone could. She was right, I did hate favors, but I'd be stupid not to take the opportunity. I was holding on to my three point eight GPA by the skin of my teeth, and med schools were fiercely competitive. If I slipped even a little, it would be hell trying to get in a good one, and I could forget about a scholarship of any sort. I had always been a fast learner, rarely having to read something more than once, but I couldn't keep up with the class work, and the diner to pay the bills, without something taking a hit.

"Are you sure?" I asked hesitantly.

Lacey let out a sigh of relief and smiled a Marilyn Monroe smile. I knew she had been practicing those. "Are you kidding? My uncle is going to be thrilled. The casinos are always looking for pretty girls. It is going to be fantastic. You'll see."

Chapter Two

"Lacey, I don't know about this." I smoothed my hand over the black satin of my new uniform. Lacey, true to her word, got her uncle to get me a job. She'd pulled some strings with her boss, who had a crush on her, to get me on her shift.

"You look stunning, what's wrong?"

"I'm naked."

"No, you aren't, silly."

"I feel like I'm going to be serving drinks in a bathing suit."

"You don't wear heels and stockings with a bathing suit. Now smush your boobs in a little so I can zip this up for you. I always thought you wore a push up bra. I can't believe how big your boobs are."

"Lacey, if you keep talking, I'm never going to be able to leave this room."

"Sorry. Come on. We've got to get out on the floor. Just try to be nice, okay?"

"I'm always nice!"

"Uh, yeah."

I couldn't have been more out of my comfort zone if I'd been wearing a big red rubber nose and a rainbow wig. My diner uniform was black pants and a white blouse and I blended perfectly into the background. I didn't want the attention an outfit

9

like this would attract.

"It feels weird to have my hair down while I'm working."

"You're serving drinks, not food. Plus, we are supposed to be attractive, not look like milk maids. And if I had hair like yours, I wouldn't put it up in that ugly ratty pony tail all the time."

"It's irritating, and it's getting too long. I'm just too cheap to get it cut."

"You're lucky you're a natural blonde and don't have to dye it all the time. God only knows how bad you'd let your roots get. You have no idea how expensive this gets to be, too," Lacey said as she pulled a lock of hair forward over her shoulder. "Now, Jonny, the bartender, is kinda creepy, but he gives me free shots when it's slow, so be nice to him."

"I know; I've got to be nice. You told me five times already."

"Ugggh."

"What? I said I'd be nice."

"No, not you. See over there?" I looked where she was pointing to the corner of the bar where the bartender, a nice looking dark Italian guy whom I guessed was Jonny, was leaning forward talking to another waitress. She looked to be in her early twenties, with black hair and a slightly Asian appearance, and was dressed like us.

"Yeah, why?"

10

"That's Vicky. She doesn't normally work this shift. She must have switched. She thinks she's boss because she's sleeping with the owner."

"She's the owner's girlfriend?" I thought it a little odd that the owner's girlfriend would be pushing drinks with the rest of us.

"No, she's not his girlfriend. She just doesn't seem to realize that, or doesn't want to."

"She's pretty. She looks kind of like Lucy Liu."

Lacey jumped in front of my path and held her hand up, eyes round as saucers. "Whatever you do, don't say that to her. She's already about to explode from the size of her ego."

"Lacey!"

We both swung around to where a bear of a man was standing about ten feet to the side of us. His hair was crazy thick and bushy, even cropped as close to his head as it was. He wore a nice suit, but he looked like a thug. He was also a complete softy and my new boss.

"Hi, Arnold," we greeted him together.

"You're both late."

"I'm sorry, Jo felt funny in her new uniform."

I gasped in indignation at being thrown under the bus so blatantly, then followed up with an elbow to her ribs.

"Like it wasn't true? You were being prudish."

I didn't say a word, not wanting to prolong the subject.

He just shook his head and sighed. "Show Jo around. And, Lacey, you have to start showing up on time."

"I'm sorry, Arnold." Lacey smiled her Monroe smile and the big bear looking thug visibly melted.

"Just try not to do it, again," he said. Lacey was late every day of the week. I knew this because she told me in the locker room just thirty minutes ago. "I need someone to run Mr. Hawking up a bottle of the scotch he likes. We're slow, so you can bring Jo with you while you show her the ropes."

"Where's Perry?"

"Lacey, can't you just do something when I ask you?"

"But that's not my job. Make Vicky do it, you know she'd be quite *happy* to." Lacey put just enough extra inflection on the word happy to make it more than obvious what she was insinuating.

"If I send Vicky, she won't come back tonight, and I can't exactly call the boss and complain. I'm already down a girl."

"Fine." Lacey stalked off in a pout, and I had no choice but to follow her having no idea what else to do. I started to remember quickly why I had no friends. I hadn't wanted any.

"What's the big deal if we run an errand?" I asked her after we had gotten out of earshot of Arnold.

12

"Because Mr. Cormac Hawking is the owner, and he makes me nervous."

She stepped up to the bar, made a face at Vicky, and introduced me to Jonny. He smiled flirtatiously, and I had the distinct impression that he would have made a move on me if Lacey hadn't sent him off quickly to go fetch the scotch for Mr. Hawking.

"Is he sleazy or something?" I asked Lacey, still wondering how somebody made her unsettled. No one unsettled her.

"No, he's actually really hot. He's just... I don't know how to explain it." She hesitated and looked back at me. "It's hard to put into words. If he's up there when we bring this, you'll see."

Jonny plunked down a bottle of scotch on the bar and threw me another smile.

"Stop looking at her like that. It's just creepy!" Lacey said as she grabbed the scotch in one hand and my arm in the other. "Don't sleep with him. He gets around and from the tally I've got, has given at least four waitresses an STD," she told me as we headed up to the private elevator that went to the private top floors. The door men that kept the general population of the casino out, held the doors for us.

We got out at the fiftieth floor. A large sumo wrestler look alike, with his sparring partner by his side, was standing in front of the elevator doors

13

when they slide open. They nodded to us as we passed.

"This floor is Mr. Hawking's only. If we were strangers, Tweedle Dee and Tweedle Dum back there, would have ripped us to pieces. I've heard there are about fifty more of their type lurking around this floor."

My heels sank into the thick cream carpet surrounded by tan walls. It was set up like a gallery, with paintings on either side, lighting above each piece of artwork.

"Is that a real Monet?" I asked, as I paused in front of oil painted water lilies. I was far from a connoisseur of art, but on my eleventh birthday, Rick, one of the foster kids who had been living at the same house I was, had given me a used book of Monet prints. I'd had to tape the binding back together last month, but I couldn't bring myself to throw it out.

"Probably, he's a huge art collector."

When we reached the end of the hallway, we came to a massive, carved wood door. The grain swirled underneath a thick coat of clear lacquer that accentuated the warmth and highlighted the skill of the artisan who had made it. Lacey reached her hand up to press the doorbell to the right, and I saw a slight tremor as her fingers hovered over the button for a moment. She pressed it, and the doors swung open before her arm had dropped back to her side.

"You have his scotch?" A tall thin blond man asked.

"Duh." She held up the bottle as if he needed visual proof. Just like the scotch, Lacey tended to be an acquired taste.

The man eyed Lacey, and then me, and stepped aside to let us in. "Put the scotch on the bar in the other room."

The moment we walked in, I felt a tingle of electricity flow over my skin, and my hair stood on end. A prehistoric remnant, left over from thousands of years ago, issued a warning that my evolved brain could no longer decipher. Combined with my lack of direction, it was hard not to wonder if evolution hadn't cut some corners along the way.

I looked over at Lacey, and when she met my gaze her eyes doubled in diameter with a blatant, *I told you I didn't want to come here. Now do you get it?*

I simply nodded and gave a silent reply to her with my eyes that said *let's drop off the bottle and get the hell out of here.*

The entire far wall of the foyer was glass, and it offered a spectacular view of the Vegas Strip. At night, like it was now, with the lights dimmed low, you could see the light going on for miles. I had a hard time breaking my gaze away from the

15

stunning view.

I followed her into the next room that looked to be the living room. It had the same outer wall of windows, with a large screen TV that somehow floated in the center. A matching set of tan suede couches faced each other and a full-length bar made of black stone ran along the back wall. My eyes searched out the view again. All I could think of was how wonderful it must be to live high up here with the world at your feet.

The apartment was eerily quiet, and we instinctively honored the silence. Somehow afraid if we uttered a word, we would draw the attention of whatever was lying in wait, the eerie presence hovering nearby that we couldn't quite define. Lacey was just about to place the bottle on the bar when we heard a rustling from the other room.

"Hello."

The deep gravelly voice sent a shiver down my spine. I looked over at the doorway to see a pair of the palest blue eyes I'd ever encountered, set like aquamarines in a frame of dark black lashes. His dark tan skin, and black wavy hair framing them, just made them even more unusual. I knew instantly that this had to be Cormac Hawking. I would have known him even in a crowded room, surrounded by hundreds of others. Lacey wasn't the type to avoid attractive men, and he was incredibly handsome in a deeply sexual way. He

16

was nicely over six feet, with broad shoulders encased in a white tuxedo shirt that hung slightly open. But it was the power that seeped from him, not his size, that made him alarming to even my senses, not that I'd ever show it, but I felt it in spades. It rolled off him in wave after wave until it practically smothered all my other senses. He was the kind of man who dominated a room without even trying. The primitive part of my brain was screaming for me to leave, but the female in me wanted to get closer, even as I knew that this man was dangerous.

I looked at Lacey to see if she was ready to make an exit, but at the current moment, she stood so still she would have made a deer in the headlights look animated.

"We were just dropping off your scotch," I stated, as Lacey remained where she was frozen.

"Thank you." He looked sparingly at Lacey, but quickly dismissed her and returned his gaze to mine. "Would you mind?" He held out his hand that had a pair of cuff links resting on his palm. "It's easier with two hands."

"Sure." He stood where he was, making me walk to him as he waited, and I think maybe assessing me. I took one link from his hand, trying to make as little contact with his skin as possible, afraid that somehow he'd discover my unease. One thing I've learned from a life of shuffling from place to place, never let them know you're nervous. Then I blew it and dropped the second link on the carpet.

"Sorry," I said, as I reached down and grabbed it.

"No problem," he replied with a smile on his lips.

I felt like he was playing a game with me, but no one had bothered to fill me in on the rules.

"Your eyes are very unusual, such a vivid green."

I met his stare fully now. I didn't like being toyed with, and some part of me knew he was playing my reactions like a fiddle.

"Thank you," I replied, and continued to hold his gaze.

"Do they run in your family?"

I hesitated, which probably seemed weird to him, being such a straightforward question. "No," I lied. Some kernel of preservation in my brain was screaming the less he knew the better. Another part of me, maybe the larger part, didn't want to admit to not knowing my parents.

He lost his smile and looked at me intently, but not aggressively. He knew I was lying. By that simple answer, I had just somehow cemented my position on his radar. He knew something was off.

He lifted his hand slowly toward my face. This game I knew well, he was playing chicken, seeing if

18

I'd stand my ground or pull back. I stood my ground and he ran his index finger along my cheekbone.

"Pretty."

His smile was back. It was a smile of a man used to winning.

"Thank you," I countered in the blasé tone of a woman used to being pursued. He was going to have to up his game if he was going to try to storm this castle. Men had chased me for months, let alone weeks, and had gotten nowhere.

The clanking sound of Lacey banging into a glass drew our notice and broke the tension.

"Sorry," she muttered softly across the room, a few shards of glass lay at her feet.

He looked unfazed. "Leave it; I'll have one of the maids get it." He turned his attention back to me. "I'm sure I'll be seeing you, again." He turned and left.

The minute he was gone, Lacey had her hand clamped around my wrist and tugged me out of there, as quickly as she could drag me.

Lacey came back to her normal self once the elevator doors slid shut, leaving the two of us alone, again. "Oh, my god!" she said. "He was so into you! I've never seen him act like that with anyone. He barely acknowledges Vicky and *he's slept with her!*"

"It's only because he's never seen me before.

19

Those kinds of men are always like that." I hoped that was what it was, because I didn't want his kind of attention. I was all about keeping my nose clean, getting into med school, and hopefully figuring out what the hell was wrong with me before NASA came and decided to find out for me. Getting derailed by some thirty something playboy, in his expensive penthouse, who wanted a little amusement wasn't what I needed. I was well past the point in my life where I believed in happily ever after. My reality didn't include castles and gallant knights, and I didn't need them. I handled my own problems. Romance and men were a luxury I couldn't afford, right now.

Chapter Three

"Hi, Jonny, I need a Bombay martini straight up with olives."

"Hi, Darling, what are you doing here?" Jonny gave me the smile he used on the girls he was working for tips, or other more personal pursuits as Lacey had informed me. He did always seem to be preoccupied, that was for sure.

"Lacey asked me to cover. She had a date tonight." I'd been there for only two weeks, and I'd already filled in for Lacey three times.

"How come you don't?" he asked shifting into full gear.

"Jonny, I don't have time to date. I told you that."

"I could take you to that nice steak house that just opened up in the Bellagio."

I didn't want to hurt his feelings, but it was hard not to laugh at his persistence. It was starting to become a routine with us. He asked. I declined. Rinse and repeat.

"Jonny, aren't you getting tired of asking?"

"Tired of asking what?" Vicky laid her tray down on the bar as she came and stood next to me. "To go out with you, again? Don't look at me all shocked. Everyone knows he's been sniffing around you nonstop for weeks."

"Why are you standing over here? Didn't you see the boss come in?" Jonny struck back at her.

"Where?" Vicky, too interested in Cormac's possible arrival, didn't even blink an eye at the dig, but instead scanned the casino floor like a hawk trying to spot her prey. "Where? I don't see him."

"You need glasses. You're as blind as a bat. He's at table seven," Jonny replied with barely concealed dislike.

I couldn't help myself, and turned to look as well. I inwardly cringed when I realized he was sitting in my area, talking to the high roller who was betting fifty thousand a hand at black jack for the last hour. Knots instantly formed in my stomach and reached all the way up to my throat. I had seen him coming and going since the night in his penthouse but always at a distance. I'd caught him watching me a handful of times, but he'd never approached me.

From what I had noticed, other than Lacey and I, most of the women here flocked to him. The very danger that made me steer clear of him, seemed to have the opposite effect, and pulled them in like magnets.

"Can I take your table? I'll give you table three. The guy's been giving me a ten every round. Please!"

She whined for a moment while I hesitated, not wanting anyone to know that I was actually

22

relieved to relinquish the table. "Okay, but you owe me." She was gone before I'd finished speaking.

"Now, back to dinner."

"Jonny, you're a nice guy, but I'm not interested. Doesn't matter who you are or how great you are, I don't date." I added the last part to try to smooth his ego. Truth was, I couldn't date. Even if I had the time and wanted to date him, which I didn't, I'd never be able to explain the weird things that happened around me. Sometimes I got tired of being alone, but that didn't change anything. I had tried dating before. Sooner or later it would get serious, and they would want to stay the night. I knew from my childhood, I couldn't risk having anyone around when I slept. That's when it got the strangest, but I couldn't think about that right now.

As I got back to checking on my section, I tried to keep my distance from table seven as much as I could. That was hard since that table sat in the middle of my area. Luckily, Vicky offered a distraction and draped herself over Cormac like a cheap suit anytime I was near. I had the distinct feeling it was because he kept watching my movements, and I wasn't the only one who had noticed. After about an hour, I started to get a little high-strung about being under constant surveillance. But, just when I'd about had it with being visually stalked, he was gone.

I was grateful, I wanted to keep this job. I'd finally been able to watch a couple of movies and have some downtime. I'd been sleeping more and even baked cookies with Mrs. Harvey. I felt like a human being again.

By time the night was done, my feet ached and I couldn't wait to get my shoes off. I hated heels and couldn't wait to get my sneakers on. Tomorrow morning, I would go for a run, another thing I had time for lately. I hadn't put on weight. I was curvy but thin. Running was simply my release from the world.

When I looked up at the bar, I saw Cormac Hawking had reappeared and was now sitting at the far end with the high roller. They looked like they were having a disagreement of sorts, and they didn't even notice me. I let out a sigh of relief that I was done for the night, and could go hide in obscurity.

"Hey, Jonny, this should be all of it," I said, as I handed him the change from the last round and a pile of singles he was going to change in for larger bills. I'd done amazingly well tonight. I'd made almost enough for half a month's rent.

When the high roller that Mr. Hawking had been sitting with approached me, I pretended to be preoccupied. The guy had been hitting on everything with legs, and I didn't feel like being the next.

"All done?" he asked

He definitely wasn't the type to take a subtle hint. I turned to see him.

"Yes," I said in a slightly clipped voice and went back to what I was doing. That was my second level rejection. In my experience, that only had a fifty percent success rate, so I wasn't surprised when he continued.

"Can I buy you a drink?"

"I don't drink." I did, but it was none of his business. He wasn't a bad looking guy, a few inches taller than my five feet four inches and solid looking with longish light brown hair. He clearly had money as well, the way he was betting, but even if I could date, and I wasn't a freak, something about him reminded me of nails on a chalk board.

"How 'bout a coffee?"

Ugh, the guy just wouldn't take the hint, or maybe you could call it a sledge hammer in this case. "I'm not interested." I could smell alcohol and a recent smoke on his breath as he moved in closer.

"I don't think you know who I am. You'd be lucky to date me."

"Right now, I'd feel lucky if you would back off, because you smell like a burned out brewery." I took a deep breath, knowing I was about to really step over the line with a customer, but the guy was starting to really piss me off. I looked up wondering where the hell Jonny had gone. I wanted to get my tips so I could get out of there, and he was nowhere to be found.

The guy reached out and grabbed my upper arm in a tight, but not painful, grip. He pulled me closer and leaned in my face, "You better ask around and learn your place quick."

Something in me snapped. I knew how I looked to people because I went out of my way to perpetrate the image. Everyone assumed a pretty little thing like me was innocent, that without a man, I was helpless. But, that was only to those who weren't looking closely enough, which luckily for me, were most. I'd spent enough time taking care of myself to handle a jerk like this.

I held his stare. "I don't know who you are, and I'm certainly not going to ask around." I leaned in as close as I could stand and whispered in a voice so low only he could hear. "And you know why? Because I don't give a shit. Now get your hand off of me, or you're going to be crawling out of here."

His grip tightened just enough to be uncomfortable. "What do you think you're going to do?" he asked.

I knew what I wanted to do, but I couldn't do that here without people knowing something wasn't right with me, but I'd learned how to get around that over the years. I'd couch what I wanted to do for something that would be almost as effective.

Kneeing a guy in between the legs works much less often than people think. Men aren't stupid about that area. It's the first place they block, so as I jerked my knee up, I knew I wasn't going to get a clean shot, but I also knew I wouldn't need one. I just had to connect to his body in that ultra sensitive area to shoot a little pain his way. No one would ever guess that anything abnormal was happening. They'd simply think I'd managed to connect better than I had.

He had no idea it was coming. One second he was leaning over me as the aggressor, and the next he was crying at my feet like a baby.

I took a step away from him, looking for Jonny, knowing it was time to flee the scene before the guy made it to his feet. When I looked around, I found quite a few people, including Jonny, had witnessed the scene.

"Thanks for the help," I said sarcastically to Jonny. I knew the next time he offered to walk me out, I'd laugh in his face.

"Didn't look like you needed any," a deep voice from behind me answered for him. With my back still to him, I grimaced slightly, then turned around, and waited to see if I was going to be fired.

I looked into Cormac's chiseled face and had no idea what he was thinking. His eyes were intense as he looked at me, and I had a fleeting thought that maybe it wouldn't be a bad thing if he fired me. Just his presence affected me more than any other man I'd ever met. "Am I fired?"

"Why would you be fired?"

Without a hint of emotion shown, I wasn't sure if he was baiting me or being obtuse. I doubted he was obtuse but I stated the obvious anyway, "Because I attacked your customer?" It was a bit awkward while the man was still lying on the ground, practically at my feet, and still occasionally moaned.

"Yes, I saw. Looked like he had it coming." He waved over a couple of men whom I hadn't noticed. "Help Tracker to his car," he told them, and they each grabbed him under the arm. "Where did you learn to take care of yourself like that?"

He was eyeing me intensely, and even though he couldn't know that there was something wrong with me, I felt like he did. I don't know how, but he knew I wasn't who I pretended to be.

"I took some self-defense classes." I'd never taken a self-defense class in my life.

He didn't say anything, just nodded his head. He knew I'd lied... again. I'd done my fair share of lying because of my secrets. I knew the tells people gave and I knew I didn't do them. I was a good liar. I was pretty confident I'd even pass a lie detector test if I had to. How did he know?

We stood there for a moment appraising each other. I waited, on the inside I was sweating bullets, waiting for him to call me a liar or ask where I'd taken a class, but on the outside I was completely poised. I stood my ground like his equal. He was the owner of the hottest casino on the strip. I'd heard whispers of him having holdings in half of the other casinos in Vegas, which was stunning for a man in his thirties. Me, on the other hand, I worried how I'd pay my rent for a trailer that looked like it's best years had come, gone, and then been forgotten. But, I didn't care.

I'd watched people tip toe around him for the last three weeks. If that was the type of employee he needed, better to fire me now. I bowed to no one.

He slowly looked me up and down. He was testing my mettle, trying to get me to shrink back, to break the silence first or bend in some telling way that would prove my inferiority. I wouldn't. What would normally be an insignificant amount of time dragged by, second after second, until he raised his eyebrows and tilted his head toward me in a silent acknowledgment. I'd passed. I didn't know exactly what I'd passed, but I'd passed. It wasn't surprising to me that I wasn't fully cued in on what had gone down. This was the second time I'd had real interaction with him. Whatever rules he lived by, I decided, were not the run-of-the-mill existence.

"I'll have someone walk you out."

"I don't need an escort."

"Buzz, walk Jo out."

I didn't ask how he knew my name, let alone my nickname. I worked for him, along with hundreds, likely thousands of others. Maybe he made it his business to know everyone. I wasn't going to make a big deal over it. I'd let his guy walk me out if he wanted to. I wasn't going to be greedy with my victories.

"I'm fine."

"I know." And as quickly as that, I was dismissed, he walked off in his own direction while his big blond brute followed me in mine.

I left Buzz at the bus stop on the strip, but I didn't feel alone until I was in my trailer, hours later.

Chapter Four

The church was deathly quiet when I walked in the next afternoon. I'd started looking for my parents the day I had turned eighteen. No one had been willing to talk to me before then. I never understood that. It was my history, I had a right to know. Turned out, there wasn't much to tell. The only thing I had found out was that a priest had dropped me off at the hospital, but no one had bothered to write his name down at the time, or perhaps they had simply lost the record.

This was the thirtieth church I'd visited. My steps echoed off the high ceilings as I walked down the aisle. I was running out of churches to go to in the area. I'd have to expand my search radius again, soon.

"Can I help you?" I turned to find a middle-aged nun behind me.

"Is your priest in? Or do you know where I could find him?"

"I'm sorry, but we aren't holding confessionals, today."

"No, I'm not here for that. Is there any chance I could speak to him?"

"I'll go see if he's available. Wait here."

I wished that my life could be simple enough to just give a confession and move on, that I could fix my problems that easily. This was one of the oldest churches I'd been to, about twenty minutes outside of Vegas. I sat down on the hard wooden pew and gazed at the afternoon sun streaming in through the stained glass windows. I could smell the age of the place, the scent of incense that had been burned over and over again still lingered in the air and I wished I could just let it all go.

I didn't even want to know these people who had given me up. They had abandoned me to a cruel world, and I had no love in my heart for them. When I had been a young girl, I would daydream of them coming and saving me. Those days were long gone. If I could walk away from this chase, I would. I didn't have that option. Every year, things got a little stranger. I was afraid of what I was becoming. The only thing I wanted from them was answers, and they'd better be ready to give them.

"Miss?" I turned to see an elderly man, probably in his mid seventies, with thin white hair. "You asked to speak to me?"

"Yes, if you have a moment? I had a couple of questions."

"Sure, what can I do for you?"

He smelled of soap and detergent, as he sat down next to me on the pew. If I hadn't been through this so many times, I might have actually felt awkward. I had initially. I'd even gotten butterflies the first few times, thinking that I might finally get the answers I craved. Now, I just felt jaded, but I started my questions, anyway.

"Did you find a baby about twenty one years ago?"

His face changed instantly, and I knew I had finally found the priest who had brought me to the hospital. He reached down and took my hand in his. I swallowed back my unease at being touched but didn't pull back.

"You're her? I remember it like it was last night. Your eyes were so unusual. I'd never forget them."

"Could you tell me what happened?"

"Yes, I still remember the night. It was a late Sunday evening in the middle of January and cold. I think it actually even broke a temperature record that day. I had just locked the doors not fifteen minutes before, and was gathering a few things, when I heard a light banging at the door. When I opened it, there was a beautiful young girl there covered in blood, with a small child not more than a year old. I let her in immediately. She was bleeding heavily from her side, so heavily that I was worried about even waiting for an ambulance. They aren't always so quick to get out this far. I left her to go grab car keys to drive her to the hospital myself. When I got back, she was gone and you were sitting on the bench crying. You were swaddled in a blanket covered with your mother's blood. I called one of the nuns, Loretta, to help me and I drove you to the hospital."

"Do you remember what she looked like?"

"She looked like you. You could've been twins."

"And she just disappeared?"

"There was so much blood, but when I looked for her outside she wasn't there. Even after I returned from the hospital, I couldn't find a trace."

"Did she say anything to you?"

He shook his head. "No, but I did find something that night. Come with me and I'll get it for you."

I stood and followed him into a back office. Shelves packed to the brim lined the walls. I was surprised they were still even clinging to the walls and hadn't crashed down from their awesome burden.

The priest was surprisingly spry for his age as he dragged a step stool across the room.

"I think it's here. Ah, yes! Here it is." He climbed down with a single sheet of paper in his hand. "It was lying on the pew right beside you."

I took the sheet and looked at it quickly.

A golden child born and left will be the hope of those bereft. When eternal lilies bloom after a torturous night, the giver of gifts will stand for the right. The one who's sought is suddenly found, it will come time to stand their ground. So comes the reckoning where many fall. Tis not the end, but the start of it all.

"Odd, right?"

The priest's voice distracted me and I looked up at him. "Yes. You really think this was left by her?"

"Yes. It was left right beside you. In the excitement of the moment, I left it behind when we went to the hospital. I kept it, figuring I'd give it to you at some point. Then days turned into weeks and years. I'd forgotten about it until you came here today."

I nodded, absorbing the fact that maybe she hadn't wanted to abandon me. For some unknown reason, it hurt worse knowing that. It had been easier to wall off those emotions behind anger than to consider perhaps I had been wanted. The strange note added to my bewilderment. It was hand written, but looked as if it had been pulled from a bond book.

"Would you like to come have a cup of tea? I've always wondered what happened to you." He reached out and grasped my hand.

I pulled back, and I saw understanding in his face. Logically, I knew he hadn't had a hand in how my life had unfolded from that point, but in my heart, I felt just as abandoned by him as by everyone else. I had no desire to retell the story of neglect and abuse, and I felt no obligation to paint a pretty picture to ease his conscience. He had been one of many who passed the buck and left an innocent child to fend for herself. Not once in the many years of my life had he come by to see if I was okay.

"Thank you for your time." I felt a twinge of remorse when I saw his face sadden, but I ignored it, just as he had ignored the baby he had dropped at the hospital.

I tucked the mysterious note into my purse and I walked out into the dry heat that came at the end of spring, but I didn't mind. I closed my eyes as I looked up and let the sun's heat sink into my skin before I walked back to the only bus stop in the area. I didn't own a car, not wanting the additional debt on top of tuition bills and rent, but I was doing so well in tips lately that I had started to consider it.

I took the bus to Lacard, not home, because I had a shift tonight. Even with all the passengers and lots of stops, I still got there an hour early, so I went to have a coffee and stroll the mall. My nerves were raw, and the priest's words buzzed in my head like an angry swarm from a disrupted hive. Was my mother dead? I'd grown up believing I was abandoned; now I didn't know what to think.

The note made no sense at all other than the golden child born and left. I was light blond, naturally golden tan and one hundred percent left.

I was gazing at the storefront, feeling akin to an emotional zombie, when I caught a glimpse of him in the reflection off the glass. He stood across the aisle, was in his early twenties, and the epitome of average, not too tall or short, not good looking, nor ugly. He was the perfect tail, or would have been if I hadn't noticed him on the bus ride over here.

I'd learned to take care of myself. That meant being aware of any possible physical threat, even if it was someone who blended into the background. There was still a chance it was a coincidence. The Lacard had the best mall on the strip nestled in its enormous walls, and it drew all sorts of foot traffic.

Trying to confirm my suspicions, I walked down a wing that carried only two stores, one lingerie and the other shoes. I discreetly glanced around and found I was alone. I ducked into the shoe store for a few moments, and pretended to be interested in a pair of boots, all the while eyeing the hallway out front. When he didn't follow, I relax a bit and then made my way back out and into the main thoroughfare. I scanned the area with my peripheral vision and inwardly cringed. I spotted him as he lingered in front of the dress store I had left. Walking slowly, I stopped and

37

paused at a cart in the center selling earrings, and I saw him start to move in my direction again but stopped when he got within twenty feet.

I looked down to check the time, I had to head in to work, or I'd be late for my shift. I held my phone up, and I tried to catch the reflection of the guy on the screen. I walked briskly and tripped. My legs swung out up in front of me and I landed in an undignified lump right in front of Godiva Chocolates. I heard a few young giggles that attested to my audience. Little jerks. What were they doing in a casino mall anyway? Didn't their parent's ever hear of Disney World?

"Are you all right?"

A male palm hovered a few feet in front of me, waiting to assist. My eyes followed the arm up to look at the well-groomed man attached. He was tall; even from my current vantage point his height was obvious. His polo shirt and khakis did little to hide the trim lean build of someone who exercised regularly, and probably had a few marathons under his belt. As a runner, I could always spot another. I waved his hand away and jumped to my feet quite smoothly.

"Yes, I'm fine. Thank you."

"I'm Vitor."

"Thanks again. Sorry, but I'm in a bit of a rush. I'm going to be late for work." I hurried off before he had a chance to ask my name. From the expression on his face, I knew it wasn't a reaction he was used to getting. It wasn't how I would normally treat someone just trying to help me, either, but my unease was growing by the minute. This was the second day in a row I felt like I'd been followed. It was becoming a bit too much for me to ignore or excuse away. I didn't want another problem, and I certainly didn't need one.

As I hurried into the back staff rooms, I felt a little of the tension release. No one but casino staff could follow here. I only had a few minutes left now before I was due on the floor, so my respite was short lived. I'd barely stepped onto the casino floor before Arnold was already calling me.

"Can you do me a favor?"

"Sure, Arnold. What do you need?" I tried to play nice with Arnold. He was the gate keeper to the best shifts, plus, I thought he was a nice guy everyone walked on.

"I've got a new girl training tonight and some guy just threw up on her. I know, gross," he said replying to my silent but strong reaction. "She's hysterical in the women's bathroom. I'll call down for it, but I need you go to laundry and inventory and pick up a new uniform for her."

"Sure, but I don't know where it is."

"Go to the basement level one. Take a left out of the elevator; make a right at the first corridor, and then the third door on the right. Thanks."

Before I could ask another question, Arnold pulled out his phone and walked away, heading toward the bathrooms.

Left, right, right I repeated to myself, wishing I had a pen to jot it down on my palm. I'd always been direction deficient. Leaving the floor, I walked to the staff elevators in the back and got in. I looked at the buttons and hit B One, that had to be it, I figured. The elevator doors opened at my selected floor to reveal all cement pathways, in stark contrast to the lush gold and red carpeting of the casino upstairs. Cinderblock walls coated in a dull grey utilitarian paint and dim fluorescent lighting above that flickered slightly gave me an eerie feeling, similar to the opening of a horror film.

I had expected to see some sort of signs, maybe a couple of arrows taped to the floor, but there was nothing. I turned, turned again, and started to count the doors to the right. When I got to the third it was locked. Maybe it was the one on the left? I counted the ones on the left and bingo, the third door opened.

All I could see were tall, box-filled shelves that climbed all the way to the ceiling. It looked like storage. There had to be some uniforms somewhere around here. "Hello?" I called out, but there was no answer, so I went farther in the room and tried to find someone. The aisles went back farther than I would have imagined, and the immense scope of the room impressed me.

A voice across the other side of the room drew my attention, so I went in that direction. "Hello?" I repeated but with no reply.

When I turned the corner, the area opened up and I could see clear to the other side of the room where a dark haired man was pinning a guy up against the wall with his forearm pressed against his throat. The guy that was pinned was the same guy I'd kneed the other night. He wasn't having a good run.

"Stay out of it! I'm going to handle it. I told you!" The dark haired man was a mere inch from the other guy's face as he spoke.

It wasn't exactly clear to me if the guy was going to choke him or if it was just a threat. The guy was a creep. Maybe he deserved what he was going to get. After I mentally debated it for a moment, I didn't think I could watch the guy kill the man who attacked me. I'm not sure what that said about me, that I'd had to think about it. Some people would have just leapt to his defense. I guess I wasn't one of those people. Nope, not really a shocking revelation.

I started looking around for a weapon of some sort to hit the one guy over the head with, when I heard a horrible growl and paused. Just wonderful, they brought a dog, too, I thought to myself. I turned to locate the furry critter, but there were only the two men still there. Then something flickering near the pinned man's face caught my eye. Bumps were breaking out and growing out of his skin. I stood and gaped at what happened next. The creep I didn't like morphed into a tall fur covered monster, complete with a muzzle full of pointy teeth.

If I hadn't been in shock, I might have just quietly run, as I didn't think either of them had noticed me. Unfortunately, that's not how things worked out. Once I saw those horrific teeth snap and growl, I screamed bloody murder. Both men instantly turned and stared at me, forgetting their own fight in the process. I belatedly turned and ran straight into what felt like a brick wall. I tried to pull away, but I was held firmly.

I looked up at the living mountain and saw that it was Buzz. He was Hawking's man; it would be okay. He was tough. Between the two of us, we could probably take them.

"Come with me," was all he said.

I eagerly preceded him from the room and didn't look back, just walked quickly away with Buzz at my back. I was too relieved to press my luck. As long as I didn't feel sharp teeth piercing me, all was right in the world.

When I headed toward the elevator, he grabbed me quickly and motioned toward the other direction. He let go of my arm as soon as I turned around so it didn't set off any alarm bells. He had been sent to protect me last night, perhaps Hawking had been the one having me followed?

"What was that thing?"

"I can't speak about it."

"You know what? That's completely okay with me. I'm just glad you showed. Those guys looked like they wanted to rip me to pieces." He didn't respond, and I didn't care. I was just happy I wasn't a bloodied mess chewed up for dinner. The one guy, or creature, or whatever he was, looked like he'd have been a tough fight in his new form. I wasn't sure my little trick would work through a thick coat of hair. I'd never zapped an animal before.

I turned to make sure we weren't being followed.

"They aren't following us. I locked the door. They won't get out until I send someone back there."

"Where we going?"

"To the top."

I looked and saw the elevator at the end of the hall. Boarding the elevator, I suspected he meant we were going to Hawking. I watched the buttons light up until it blinked on the top level, Hawking's level. I didn't realize it initially, but this must be Hawking's private elevator.

The doors opened to the familiar tan hallway of art, but this time the penthouse door opened for us as if on cue. The butler type person didn't speak, just shook his head, shut the door after us, and left the room.

A muscular man in his mid thirties, the type you would expect to see at Gold's Gym, came out of the living room area. He was tall and muscular like Hawking, but without any of the refined feeling to offset it. He seemed a bit brutish, closer to the impression Buzz gave. He had very dark hair, but it was brown, not the true black of Hawking's.

"What's this?" he asked Buzz.

"She saw Tracker change," Buzz replied.

Right then and there I got a sinking feeling in my gut. He hadn't been saving me at all. On the outside, I played it cool, but on the inside, I was shooting off a list of expletives that would do the most jaded streetwalker proud. After all these years, I knew better.

"Can I use the bathroom?" I asked, trying to act dumb. They both looked at me and shook their heads in unison. Okay, so they weren't as stupid as they looked I guess. I scanned the foyer, but there was nothing I could use as a weapon. I'd never had to take on two men at once. I guess today I'd see how special I really was. Was I X-Men special, or just a little different? You know, in the movies they always learned about their powers slowly. God my life sucked.

"Why did you bring her here?" the guy asked.

"Cormac had me watch her the other day. I didn't want to just handle it without checking. I got a weird vibe that he liked this one."

Okay, whatever they planned, they wouldn't do it without Hawking. I'd gotten the same vibe. I wasn't sure if wanting me in his bed was exactly something to take to the bank, but it was better than nothing. Cormac was in charge. He wouldn't let these people kill me, even if he didn't want to sleep with me. I mean, that would just be insane. No one does that.

"You better bring her in, then. I'll go get him."

"Thanks, Dodd," Buzz said to the other man's retreating back, and then he waved me in the direction of the other room.

We were alone in the foyer. It might be the best odds I'd get. I'd never be able to get away from three of them, so I lunged at him and concentrated on my hands. I didn't know exactly what happened when I did this, but it was usually painful for the other person.

I stood there, hands on his chest but he wasn't moving. Looking up, I saw Buzz looked down at my hands. I felt a deep rumbling in his chest before his laughter broke the silence.

"Not going to work," was all he said.

I dropped my arms to my side, a tad

embarrassed. "I had to try."

"Of course." He held out his hand and pointed me toward the next room.

Hawking entered the room less than a minute after us, and our eyes met and held.

"Mr. Hawking?" I asked, the question clear in my voice. I didn't say the words, but the need was there. It was as close to begging as I would ever get in my life.

When he broke eye contact first to look at Buzz, the knot in my stomach grew larger. I didn't know if he would do it, but he could, and that scared the shit out of me.

"Are you a hundred percent sure?" he asked Buzz.

I eyed the distance to the doorway and Buzz repositioned himself in front of it. They knew I'd never get past them. Not alive, anyway. I looked around the room, searching for any possible escape route.

"Sorry, boss, but I'm a thousand percent."

The room fell deadly quiet as Hawking walked toward the wall of windows and all three of us watched his back. I knew my life, or death, was being decided as we waited.

"I don't know who you are, or what, but if you kill me, there will be a herd of people coming for you." Other than the Harvey's and Lacey, I wasn't sure anyone would even know I was gone, let alone a bloodthirsty hoard seeking vengeance.

"If we don't do it, you know what we'll have to deal with. Not to mention, it might be kinder this way," the man named Dodd interjected, sensing the wavering in Hawking.

"Could my day get any worse?" he said to the room in general.

"Really? You're complaining about your day?" I responded.

Hawking smiled at me, but it was more of the bittersweet variety. "You've got a lot of spunk," he said.

He turned his back and stared out the window, his body going deathly still, then a burst of motion as he punched a perfect hole through the glass window. I knew my fate had just been sealed, as I looked at the bloodied hole he'd left behind. He didn't say anything, and he wouldn't look at me, just nodded his head and walked from the room.

"Sorry, but this is much larger than you," Dodd said apologetically in my direction.

"Fuck you," I replied calmly.

He didn't seem fazed at all, just gave me a sad smile, like he regretted this as well, but not enough to save me from the fate I'd just been dealt.

He shook his head, as he eyed me up and down. "What a waste. Make it quick Buzz."

I looked at Buzz and saw the gun he now

aimed at my head.

"You better hope that there isn't an afterlife because I'll haunt your every last step." I refused to cry or grovel. If this was the end, then so be it. I'd lived a tough life, and there was no way I'd spend my last minutes groveling to these assholes.

The last thing I heard was a gunshot. My last feeling was exploding pain, like nothing I'd ever experienced in my life. And then nothing.

Chapter Five

The crippling pain was the first thing that made me realize I was alive. I refused to believe there were headaches like this in Heaven. Unless I'd ended up at a more southerly locale? Could happen. I had been far from a saint.

Then I felt Hawking's couch beneath me. No, I was alive. Did that idiot just graze me? At least they could have given me the courtesy of killing me correctly. The pounding in my head was beyond severe, I didn't even want to open my eyes, but I couldn't ignore the shouting that was happening around me.

"What do you mean she's alive? What's the matter with you? You can't even shoot straight?" Thank you, Dodd. That's exactly what I would have said to the big dope. "Just shoot her again, you idiot."

"You think I didn't try that? That I've been sitting out here whistling Dixie? I shot her five times! She goes dead for about two minutes then the god damn bullets push out of her head."

Blessed silence fell over the room, for all of two minutes.

"Oh, my god, you moron, she's one of us. She's a Keeper! Humans don't spit bullets back out! I gotta go get Cormac. This isn't good."

I wondered what wasn't good, that I'd made it? Or that they'd shot me? And what on earth did they mean by saying I was a keeper? It sounded like a name, not just like, eh, let's keep her.

I'd never had such a headache in my life. I tried to squint my eyes open slightly, but the light did me in, and I shut them quickly. The contents of my stomach churned with the pain.

"Get me a bucket," I whispered. I wasn't sure why I cared about throwing up all over their rug. Maybe it was habit. I felt too sick to think about my motivations.

"What?"

"Bucket!" I said, as I leaned on my side, my arm hanging over the edge of the couch.

I felt the coolness of the metal slide next to my hand a second before I leaned over and emptied my stomach. The pain shot at the backs of my eyes, and then I leaned back and moaned. I prayed that now they would shoot me.

I felt a warm large hand reach down and grab my wrist, and I tugged it back abruptly. I hated being touched, and I certainly didn't want to have any of these men touch me. He grabbed me again and held firmer. I wasn't sure how I knew, but I was positive it was Hawking. I felt his fingertips feeling for my pulse.

Even as my head pounded, I couldn't stop the sarcasm from dripping out, "Clearly, I'm alive."

He ignored me, and kept his fingers at my pulse.

"I want a blood sample done, and I want the results back within the hour," Hawking said.

"Who do you think did it?" Dodd asked.

"Whoever it was, they probably didn't know. Why would they hide it? There would have been no reason not to register her." I felt a pinch at my elbow but couldn't pull away, because Hawking had a firm grasp on my wrist.

"Stop pulling. You're just going to make the needle jab you."

I pulled even harder.

"Stop," Hawking said. I opened my eyes as I felt a weight press on my chest to see Buzz sitting partially on top of me.

"Get off of her," I heard Hawking say, or perhaps growl might be a better description of the tone, and Buzz quickly jumped off.

"How old are you?" Hawking asked.

"None of your business."

"That's all right. I'll find out anyway."

I didn't bother replying. Just pretended he hadn't spoken.

I looked over and saw Hawking remove a needle from my vein and I yanked my arm back again, and this time he let go.

"Dodd, look up Josephine Davids on our system," Hawking ordered.

I tried to push myself upright, but had to stop midway as the searing pain that the movement brought crippled me. If I wasn't so miserable, I might even laugh. Let them look me up. I sat there and waited.

"There's nothing here," Dodd said.

Thank you, Oslo. Once I turned eighteen, the first thing I had done was buy myself a new identity from Oslo. I'd needed a clean break from my past. I'd met some unsavory people in my life and a few of those people had known something was off. I didn't want to leave a trail. Oslo, I didn't know his last name, had created a new identity for me. It had been worth every saved penny I'd had.

Cormac left the two guys hunched over the computer, and sat next to me on the couch. Wearing black slacks and a dress shirt, partially unbuttoned and rolled up at the wrists, he looked as handsome as he had the other night, but now instead of admiring his looks, I wanted to stab him in the heart with the first thing I could find that would get the job done.

"I know you're angry." He was speaking to me as if I were a wayward child, not a person he had just ordered killed.

"You're a bright one, aren't you?" The loathing was clear in my voice.

"When Buzz shot you, we didn't know you were one of us."

Which was what? Here was someone that could finally give me some answers, and I'd kill him before I'd admit I wanted anything from him. I sat there silently and refused to even to look at him.

"I didn't have a choice."

That shocked a response from me. "That's a cop-out. You always have a choice." I looked at him now and hoped my disgust was as clear and evident as I felt it.

His pale blue eyes looked back at me. I'd never seen eyes of such a pale blue. I also saw hardness, or perhaps cynicism, in them.

"You see things in black and white because you're young."

"Don't you even try to lecture me. You just had someone try to kill me for doing nothing. If not understanding that is a fault of youth, then you can keep the wisdom you gained in that extra ten years, Mr. Older and Wiser. You're a joke."

Any softness I thought I had glimpsed quickly disappeared. He stood and looked at me now with harshness. "I wish I had the option of making choices only for myself. I can't be that selfish. Maybe when you grow up you'll understand that."

"Yes, when I hit thirty and I know it all, I'm sure I'll understand, then."

"Don't you even want to know what you are? Or are you too stubborn to even admit that you're clueless?" he asked. He was staring at me intently and it was making every cell of my being feel more alive and intense than I'd ever felt in my life. That made me hate him even more.

"I know exactly what I am." I looked across the room, staring at the expanse of Vegas in its fully lit glory.

"You have no idea. And what's worse, you'll sit here in ignorance rather than temper your pride," he said scornfully, still watching me. "Your records before age eighteen are nonexistent. What's your real name?"

I started to fidget and stopped myself, but I couldn't stop my palms from sweating or from breathing erratically. I'd always had nerves of steel, but I had just reached my maximum. "I'm not staying here all night with you. Either shoot me, again, or let me go. Since you people can't even seem to kill a person correctly, it might be easier just to let me go. Unless of course you want to try bungling it a few more times?" I could feel my control slipping. I needed to get away from here before I lost it completely.

The jerk had the nerve to laugh at my last comment.

"I can't just let you walk out of here. I can't have you repeat what you saw."

"I won't." I jumped at the sliver of hope and was instantly annoyed with myself. He was probably just toying with me. I stood uneasily, and slowly made my way over to the window on shaky legs. I stared at the lights of Vegas that always called to me. I needed to get my nerves under control. My head was pounding so hard, it was difficult to think straight.

"Perhaps you won't. I have a feeling you don't say much to anyone. I'm having your blood run now to confirm what I think you are. When that comes back, we'll discuss what is going to happen." He turned back to Buzz and Dodd who were still standing next to the computer on the other side of the large room. I didn't know if they'd been listening, but I suspected they had.

"Dodd, get the sample taken care of. Buzz, go make sure that the other issue is handled and make our apologies," Hawking told them.

I watched them leave, and I knew I was alone in the place with Hawking. I wasn't sure if this improved my odds, or worsened them, because of all the people I'd ever met in my life, he rattled me worse than anyone. That said a lot. I'd met some pretty bad people.

"Do you want to take a shower?" he asked now that we were alone.

My knee jerk reaction was that he had just sexually propositioned me. Then I caught a glimpse of a bloodstain in the reflection of the window, and I realized what I looked like. I lifted my hand to my hair and felt clumps matted together. I looked down and saw that my blood had caked on the skin of my chest, and for the first time, I realized that they had really shot me. How was I even alive? I felt for a gash in my head, but there was nothing. I clearly remembered the shooting pain right before I blacked out. My hands started to tremble uncontrollably, and I felt like I couldn't catch my breath.

"Josephine, come, sit down." He started toward me with his palms up and outspread, trying to keep me calm as he approached.

I moved farther away from him, and whirled around, panicked. Then I saw the couch I had just been sitting on, it was covered in blood, my blood. I heard screaming and realized quickly it was coming from me, but I couldn't stop.

Hawking's arms wrapped around me from behind as he pulled me back into a hard embrace. I tried to pull away, but he didn't budge. He just held me tight against his chest and turned me away from the bloodied couch, the final trigger of what appeared to be my emotional breakdown.

"It's okay," he whispered in my ear, over and over again.

I don't know how long we stood like that, but as I started to get a grip on myself, I realized the absurdity of being comforted by my executioner. His embrace loosened as my breathing became controlled, and I pulled out of his arms.

"Don't touch me." I wrapped my arms around myself and stood with my back to him, wiping my nose and eyes, as I tried to rid myself of any trace of a breakdown.

"You'll feel better if you shower. I'll get you a change of clothes." He sounded like he was a few feet behind me, but I didn't want to look.

"I don't need anything from you, and stop telling me what you think I should do." I turned back to him now and put as much weight behind my next words as I could, "Because I don't care what you think or who you are." My situation was a disaster, but at least I sounded calm and in control again. "You ordered my death. I don't even want to hear your voice. I don't care why you made your choice. You did, that's all that matters. You say your world is complicated, that's an excuse. You are a monster."

He slowly stalked me across the room, and I found myself taking several steps backward until I felt the wall at my back. He stopped just short of touching me, but close enough that his shirt grazed my chest, his hands braced on either side of my head.

"My choices are larger than you," his voice was deadly soft as he spoke and a chill spread across my skin. "If by killing you, I protect thousands of others, then that's the choice I'd make. Every. Single. Time. And I won't apologize for it. You'd better wise up real quick, because you don't want to go toe to toe with me. You won't stand a chance."

"We'll see about that." It came out before I even knew what I was saying, but my pride had taken enough of a beating. I was done backing down.

His whole body tensed as it hovered around me. I could feel the energy pouring off him and I sucked in a breath, afraid to move an inch. Afraid of what I would unleash if I so much as grazed him. It took every ounce of nerve I had to hold my ground and not back down. We stood frozen, the tension thick. He lifted his hand, slammed it against the wall, and then he left. I stayed exactly where I was, afraid if I left the support of the wall at my back, I'd fall to the floor.

Chapter Six

It took me all of five minutes to gather my wits once he left the room and to run for the door. The tall lanky man that had let us in was back in place. He was standing firmly in front of the door, and we eyed each other.

"I know what you're thinking, and you're probably right," he said. "You might make it past me, but there are about twenty other men that look significantly scarier than I do that you'd have to get past, so good luck with that."

I stared at him, undaunted by what lay before me. Okay, maybe not undaunted exactly, but it was my only shot of busting out of there.

A chirping sound suddenly echoed through the hall and I realized it was his phone ringing. "Could we put this attack on hold for one moment?"

"Oh, yeah, sure, take your time. I wouldn't want to interrupt your phone call with our fight to the death or anything," I replied, as I made a show of leaning against the wall and crossing my ankles.

"Thank you," he said to me as he answered. He must have said yes five times before he ended the phone call, his eyes never leaving mine. "Mr. Hawking has asked me to inform you, that you are not to leave this apartment, and most certainly not covered in blood as you are. That he has five men outside of this door who will drag you back in if you try. He suggests you try to be rational for a moment, and let me show you to the guest suite, where you can shower and change. If you refuse, he will have to force the issue, as he cannot have you walking around his casino as is, and given his current temper, he prefers not to do that at the moment."

He could be bluffing, maybe there wasn't anyone outside the door, but I doubted that. I'd seen his men appear out of nowhere more than one time on the casino floor. This was his private domain. He had priceless works of art hanging on the walls in the hallway; of course there would be security. I wanted out of there, but I couldn't be stupid about it either. There was no way I'd make it out right now.

"Show me the way," I said resignedly.

"If I may say so, I believe you are making the correct choice," he said as he walked past me and in the opposite direction of the living room. I was happy I'd at least be on the opposite side of the apartment.

"Considering that you are working for a man who kills innocent people, I don't care what you think."

"I can understand that, but no matter how Cormac appears, he is an honorable man"

"I said I'd stay, not that I'd listen to you tell me what a great man he is. If you say another word about him, I'm walking out of here, five big goons or not."

To his credit, he didn't mutter another word and didn't seem to take offense either. I didn't hear the lock click when he shut the door, but what was the need?

The bedroom suite was stunning, and larger than the trailer I lived in. It was all muted tans like the rest of the apartment. A huge king sized bed sat in the middle of the room, with a tufted suede headboard, incredibly thick carpet underfoot, and an enormous flat screen TV. The far wall was all glass, like it was in the rest of the apartment, with the Vegas Strip on display. It had everything you could want, but I still didn't want to be there.

I walked into the private bathroom, decorated in polished tan marble. It was beautiful, with a large vanity, and a Jacuzzi I would have died for on any normal day, unfortunately, today had been anything but normal.

I couldn't avoid my reflection in the large mirrored wall that sat over the vanity area. I looked worse than I had imagined. There was blood caked so thick it was obvious even against the black satin of my outfit, and my hair, also, was caked in blood. I had grey smudges of mascara streaked down my face. I guess that's what you get for buying the

61

cheap makeup. Next breakdown I'd be sure to wear waterproof.

After I checked that the bathroom door locked, I stripped down and I turned the shower on until the heat of the water sent shivers through me. I worked as quickly as I could to get the blood from my hair and body, jumping every time I thought I heard a noise, constantly waiting for someone to barge in trying to shoot me, again. But when I got out, I dreaded putting on my bloody outfit.

I was still trying to wrap my head around what had happened. Being shot in the head is traumatic, even if you walk away unscathed. Plus, I didn't feel unscathed. I felt battered. My head had finally stopped pounding, but it didn't seem to help me think any clearer. I'd known horrible people, oh hell, I'd lived with horrible people, but I'd never been shot in cold blood like that.

Wrapped in the largest bath towel I'd ever seen, I listened at the bathroom door, making sure no one was in the bedroom before I went in. When I stepped into the room, there was a pair of designer jeans, a cream-colored sweater, undergarments, and even shoes laid out on the bed, everything new with tags.

I didn't want to take anything from this man, but I didn't want to put my bloody clothes back on, either, and think of what they represented. I'd also make a much easier target in clothes covered in blood. I mean, really, how loud did I want to scream, "Here I am", as I was trying to flee.

The clothes were better quality than anything I'd ever owned. The jeans alone cost more than my rent for a month. The sweater felt like cashmere and the boots were Italian leather.

After I finished dressing, I slowly opened the bedroom door, walking on tiptoes to avoid making a sound; I made my way across the foyer. His doorman, or whatever he was, was gone. This was just too easy I thought, as I pulled the front door open.

"Can we help you?" There were four wrestler looking men all staring down at me.

"I thought there were five of you guys?"

"Jimmy's down the hall. Would you like us to get him for you?"

"Nope, just wanted to make sure you weren't slacking."

I shut the door and leaned against it. I wanted to bang my head against the wall, but the headache had just started to subside.

Then I heard a tongue clucking, as Cormac's doorman came strolling around the corner, shaking his head.

"What?"

"Mr. Hawking is waiting for you in the living room."

"Let me just run right in there, then. I wouldn't want to keep my killer waiting."

As I walked away, I swear I heard him chuckling.

Cormac stood at the bar, his pale blue eyes met my green as I walked into the room. Dressed in the same black slacks, but a new pewter grey shirt, it made me wonder if some of my blood had gotten onto him. He stood with a sheet of paper in his hand.

"You summoned?" I said, as I threw myself onto the couch that wasn't covered in my blood. I avoided looking directly at the one that looked like a crime scene. I'd gotten myself under control, and I didn't want to chance another breakdown.

"I see you're faring better?" he asked with a raise of an eyebrow.

"Now that I don't have someone shooting bullets in my head, yes, I do feel better," I replied in a calm and controlled voice. "Now, what do you want?"

I saw what I thought was the beginning of a smile tugging at the corner of his lips. I couldn't be sure, but I got the impression I amused him.

"I'm going to let you leave here, but there are conditions that are nonnegotiable."

"Which are?" There had to be a catch. I was having a hard time believing that he was going to let me just stroll out of there after everything that happened. Then again, maybe he would? Who'd believe I'd been shot in the head five times and was fine? That certainly wasn't something I wanted to own up to, but if he was willing to kill me for seeing some freak turn into a monster, what had changed?

"You will not speak a word of what happened. I made excuses to your floor manager, Arnold. He won't ask what happened to you tonight. You will continue to work here and go on with life as usual." He walked over and laid a piece of paper on the table in front of me, with a fancy pen beside it. "This is a letter of nondisclosure. It also states that you will not leave the Vegas area without giving notice."

"And that's it? I sign this, and you let me walk out of here?"

"Yes." He sat down on the other end of the couch and I could smell the scent of him as he passed me.

This had to be a set up. It was too easy. I scanned the sheet, which was simplistic in its wording and style. It only had two lines. The first stated I wouldn't disclose any of the actions that had occurred in the last twenty-four hours. The second statement explained that I would agree to accept whatever consequences if I did break the contract.

I had nothing to lose and everything to gain at

this point. I reached down to sign the paper quickly, and he grabbed my wrist and halted me. The connection tingled where our skin touched and I wondered what exactly he was, and for that matter, what that made me. I had a bad feeling it wasn't something I was going to like.

"This is a binding contract. If you renege, there will be repercussions."

"Like what? Are you going to shoot me a sixth time?" I'd always had a hard time with sarcasm. People told me I used it as a defense mechanism. I disagreed. I just thought I was funny.

I pulled my wrist free and signed. "Red ink, fitting. Considering the situation, I'm surprised that you didn't make me sign in blood." I laid the pen down near the paper.

He didn't answer, just took it off the table, folded it and put it in his pocket.

"I can leave now?"

"You're free to go."

I hesitated, now that I could walk out the door I knew I left behind any possible answers about my origin that I might have been able to discover. I stood, taking longer than what I naturally would have. Angry that I hadn't gotten the answers when he had offered.

"Did you need something else?" He looked to me, his face blank, but I could sense amusement again. He knew what I wanted but clearly wasn't going to make it easy for me.

My spine straightened. I'd figure it out on my own. "I don't need anything," I said, as I walked from the room.

My hand was on the knob closing the door when I heard him. "By the way, you're an alchemist." The door clicked in place.

So I'm an Alchemist? What the hell did that mean?

Chapter Seven

I groaned when I heard Mrs. Harvey knock the next day. Looking at my beat up clock it was four in the afternoon, give or take ten minutes. I'd slept over twelve hours. Sometimes I couldn't sleep for more than three, so I was shocked. I guess even though I had healed, getting shot multiple times still took some recuperating.

When I finally made it home last night, I'd spent a good few hours researching Alchemists. All I'd found was a bunch of rubbish about changing base metals into gold and the fountain of youth. Nothing even came close to jiving with what I'd experienced. Plus, I hadn't been able to lose the feeling I'd been followed, even though I hadn't seen anyone.

Standing up, I was in boy shorts and a thin t-shirt minus a bra, but I didn't think she'd care, so I went to go greet her as is, but it wasn't Mrs. Harvey when I opened the door. I knew his face. He had introduced himself as Vitor. It was the man who had asked me if I was okay after I'd fallen at Lacard.

"What are you doing here?" I held the thin aluminum door firm, ready to slam it in his pretty face if I needed. It would probably buy me all of two minutes.

He held up his palms in the universal sign of surrender. "I mean you no harm. I just want to talk."

"You've been following me." I didn't need it confirmed, but he nodded anyway. He wasn't as large, or filled out as Hawking, but he still had a powerful build. If he was immune to my tricks, like Hawking's men had been, I wouldn't stand a chance at a one on one fight against him. "Why?"

"Can I come in and talk to you?"

If I let him in, he could do god knows what to me. If I didn't let him in, he'd probably still do god knows what to me. I glanced over at the Harvey's and saw there wasn't a single light on. They had bad eyes, so even in the middle of the day they would keep a light on. They were probably at bingo. No one else would even call the police if they saw me dragged off, not in this neighborhood. In this place, you minded your own business, or you would be next on the list. I decided at the last minute to try to play nice, or as nice as I was capable of being. I stood back and waived him in.

"Wait here, I'll be back in one minute." I walked down the hall to my room and found a pair of sweat pants and a sweatshirt. I took it as a good sign he hadn't tried to follow me.

When I walked back into the living room, it was almost funny how out of place he looked, in his expensive shirt and slacks, sitting on my plaid hand me down couch that had holes at the ends of the arms. Some people might have been uncomfortable about it, not me. I didn't ask him to come. If he didn't like my place, I was quite happy for him to leave. I stayed standing near the door, and eyed him warily.

"Well? What do you want?"

"Josephine, I was hoping to get to know you slowly. Give us some time to establish a relationship and trust, before I had to broach this subject with you, but after last night, I don't feel like I have that luxury anymore."

"What do you know about last night?" I asked.

"I know that you were on your shift and then disappeared, later to be seen leaving the penthouse elevators. I can only assume that you were with him."

"And why is that a problem?"

"I'd like you to hear my side of things before you choose."

I let that soak in for a moment. Why would he think I'd be on Cormac's side? Why would Cormac even want me on his side? But, at least this meant he wasn't in cahoots with Hawking. "And what is your side?"

"I would think my side would be obvious."

I watched my words as I answered. I wasn't clear on what constituted a break in the contract, and I didn't know what the ramifications would be.

70

Not that I was sure I was going to honor it, but if I did break it, I thought it might be a good idea to know. "Why don't you just humor me," I said.

I watched him as I waited for his reply. He wasn't just handsome, he looked kind. He might have been more handsome than Hawking, but where Hawking's presence put me on edge, Vitor had a face that put me at ease. That wasn't necessarily a good thing. I knew Hawking for what he was. He didn't make any apologizes. Vitor was still an unknown. I couldn't let angelic looks lull me into a false security.

"I'm with my people. I'd never go against the Fae. Did he tell you I would?"

Stay calm. Must stay calm and keep him calm. "No, he didn't say anything of the sort. I just wanted to hear it from you. After all, I don't know you or where your loyalties lie. I don't know why you expect me to help."

"I know you have no reason to want to."

"But?" I asked, while my mind figured it could at least check Fae off the list.

"My people need help and Cormac Hawking refuses to allow them to come to Earth."

Whoa, now! Earth? This dude was a freaking alien? This was even stranger than I had initially feared. Stay calm. Hiding my feelings was something I used to be a pro at but, wow, these people were giving me a run for my money today.

71

When I somehow managed not to give any reaction he continued, "The power he has greatly affects many lives, and where he could allow free access, he withholds it. I'd even go as far as saying he hoards it and many suffer. The resources of my people are greatly depleted."

"And if you came here? Wouldn't it just happen again? We've got our own problems."

"It wouldn't happen here. We've learned. We know how to avoid doing the same thing. We have technologies that could make your lives better."

"Then why don't you fix your own planet."

"We've tried, but it's too late. There are things that were done that are irreversible."

"I still don't see what this has to do with me? This is between you and him as far as what I've heard." Which, in reality, was nothing up until now.

"It might be now, but it won't remain that way."

I walked toward my door and pulled it open.

His face took on a saddened appearance, and I wasn't sure if it was an act or on purpose.

"I understand your bitterness. I know what your life has been like."

"Go ahead, tell me what you know about my life." I'd meant for that to sound confident. I'd meant to shut him down. I knew there were no paper trails of where I'd come from, but when the words came out, they rang of defensiveness.

72

"You're right. I don't know any of the facts, but I do know things. I know that whatever happened to you, it damaged you so much you're afraid you'll never be normal. That you can't stand to be touched; so much so that you throw off a repellent you aren't even aware of. That you are still trying to..."

"Get out!"

"Josephine, I'm sorry, I was just trying to..."

I didn't give him a chance to finish, as I abandoned my own home. My hands had begun to shake again, and I sprinted away with every ounce of energy I possessed. I'd been holding it together for my entire adult life and most of my childhood. I refused to have a second breakdown less than twenty-four hours from the first.

Winded, my legs burned with built up lactic acid, and I paused, looking behind me. My trailer park was nothing but a glittering spot on the horizon, ahead of me, nothing but the desert dunes as the sun started to make its final decent of the day. I felt alone. It was what I needed. It was what I knew. Alone was how I would pull the pieces back together.

Chapter Eight

It was the first time I was going back to the casino for work since the infamous night of my death, or as it turned out, deathlike experience. I'd packed and unpacked my bags at least ten times in the last day, but I had too much at stake to start over, again. If I picked up and left now, I would need another new identity. I would have to redo years of schooling just when I was so close to being finished. I had to hang in there for a little longer.

Another part of me, the one who had started to calm down and think logically, realized I had finally found a source of answers and wanted to stay. If I ran now, I might never know. The whole reason I had even wanted to become a doctor was now within my grasp. Only problem was the same logical part of me knew that although Hawking might have the answers, he'd also tried to kill me. Who knew when he might think it was a good idea to do it again. In his world, I was dispensable.

Even now, I knew I was being tailed everywhere I went. I felt it, even if I couldn't always spot it. A new work uniform was waiting by my door when I got up this morning. They all knew my address, which was not the one listed on my application or my college record. All my mail went to a post office box. Perhaps it was time to find a

74

new residence. I'd have to check into that online after work tonight.

I dreaded going in tonight, but it seemed strangely normal once I started. I had made it halfway through my shift, and had psyched myself up enough that I started to believe I was going to be able to do this. The fact that no one seemed to know anything had happened helped me fool myself into the thought that this would turn out okay.

I saw Hawking in passing, a few times. Other than a look that seemed to linger longer than it should have, he didn't even acknowledge me. That didn't get me the information I wanted, but I didn't feel like I'd have to run for my life anytime soon, either.

"Hey, Jo, since we're slow, do you want to cut out early? If you want to stay, I'll ask Vicky," Arnold said to me a while later, as I hung around the service bar.

"I'll go. Thanks." I was relieved to get off the floor. I'd waited for something to happen all night. Even when everything had gone smoothly, I was exhausted from the anticipation of waiting for something that had never materialized. I'd go home and relax on my couch, and read up for my finals.

I quickly changed and went to wait for the bus that would take me home. I felt the tingling sensation of being watched again as I stood at the stop. This time I had the feeling it was Hawking. I'd slipped out the back entrance that only a casino person would've been able to see me leave. He was probably watching to make sure I held up my end of the bargain. I was, at least for now. I needed information from him, and I wouldn't completely burn that bridge until I had it. Once I had what I needed, I planned to take a blow torch to it. He had me shot, I might not have died, but I was still prickly about it. That wasn't something I was going to get over. In fact, my anger had done nothing but grow in the last day. He would be lucky if I didn't torch the whole casino down around him. I might be a broke waitress, right now, but I was resourceful. I'd find a way.

I spent the ride home thinking about how satisfying it would be to take Hawking down. I was so immersed in my thoughts I almost missed my stop. I pulled the cord and had to get out a block farther away than normal, but it was a beautiful night for a walk, and I figured the guy following me should earn his keep. Let him have to hop from bush to bush for all I cared.

I couldn't pin-point anyone on the bus who looked like a tail, and when I got off, I got off alone. My best guess was that whoever was following had driven behind in a car. Apparently, these thugs had higher standards then I did and wouldn't slum it on public transportation.

The bus had just pulled away when a man stepped into my path. I looked up to see Vitor's face. I just shook my head and walked around him.

"How are you, Jo?" he asked, as he fell into step beside me.

"I've been better," I replied without bothering to look at him.

"I saw you at the casino. I think I misjudged whatever happened the other night. You aren't on the best terms with Cormac. I'm not exactly sure why you are so opposed to hearing me out."

"Because you want something from me, and whatever it is, I want no part of it."

"Why won't you at least hear me out? Maybe we could help each other."

I couldn't help myself, I had to laugh at that. "I don't need anything from you that badly, and I have a feeling whatever I could gain would cost me a lot more than I was willing to give." As we walked into my development, I headed toward my trailer. He already knew where I lived, so I didn't see the point in evasion now. And for whatever reason, I didn't think he was a threat.

"I have information that I think you would want to know."

We stopped in front of my trailer, and he held his hand on my door. I was forced to pause, whether I wanted to or not.

"What?"

"There are whispers, Josephine. Something is coming, something big that will steam roll over Cormac's entire organization. You are one of them. Do you want to take that chance?"

"What's coming?"

"There are dangerous people aligning against Cormac and they aren't alone."

"Shouldn't you be telling him?"

"He won't do what needs to be done. I need you. "

"I've told you, I'm sorry your people are having trouble, but I learned years ago that there is only one person you can depend on. Maybe it's time for them to learn that lesson, too."

I looked meaningfully at his hand and stood waiting for him to remove it.

"You're backing me into a corner, Jo."

The sound of desperation in his tone alarmed me. I looked at his face now, and realized that I might have been lulled into a false sense of security with him. It wasn't in his nature to attack, of that I was positive, but he was desperate. Desperation made people do horrible things. I'd seen it many times in my life.

I tried to soften my face and body language. "Look, Vitor, I'm really beat tonight. How about tomorrow afternoon we sit down and talk? I promise I'll hear you out then."

His hand relaxed on my doorknob. I'd walked him back from the cliff just enough to buy me the time I needed.

"Okay," he said, then paused as if figuring out his schedule in his head. "I'll be here at three."

"Deal."

He nodded his head, and I watched his back as he walked away. When he was willing to take my word on the meeting tomorrow, he proved he was honest. Only honest people take you at your word. Liars and thieves expect the same in return. Unfortunately for him, I didn't have a problem lying when it came to saving my own ass.

I went inside, opened up my laptop and typed a quick email to my professors. I wrote that there had been a death in the family. I'd dummy up the documents if it meant they'd let me finish my course at a later time. Either way, a degree wasn't worth my life. Whatever was going on, I didn't know, but the visit from Vitor had just tipped my hand. I needed to get out of here and I needed to do it now.

Hawking wasn't someone I was ready to go against, and I wasn't letting anyone pull me into a fight with him. I'd take on Hawking when I was prepared to, not because I was being forced to. I wasn't prepared to willingly go to him for help either. That would constitute choosing sides. Me, myself, and I didn't leave room for sides. One thing

I knew for sure, if I didn't choose, I wasn't ready for the hell that was about to come my way if I stuck around.

I packed everything I could get into a duffle bag and waited. And waited. Finally, at three forty-five a.m., I made my move. I crawled out the back window of my trailer and made a slightly undignified thump on the ground. I stayed low and in between the trailers until I made my way out through the back of the development.

Constantly checking every shadow, I was pretty sure I'd made a clean break. I ducked into the twenty-four hour Seven Eleven, and bribed the clerk with a five to use his phone. Using my cell phone was out of the question. I wouldn't put it past Cormac to have it bugged, so it was turned off, lying useless in my bag. Hawking had plenty of money, and Vitor didn't look like a slouch in that department, either, if the Rolex he'd been wearing tonight was any indication. Money usually meant plenty of connections. Who knew what either of them might be able to gain access to when they tried.

I had the cab pick me up a block away, not wanting any witness to the taxi company I used. I thought it would be better not to take the cab too far out of the area either, more traceable that way, but there wasn't a bus that ran along this line this time at night.

I hopped into the shabby interior of the cab. "Take me to the nearest major bus depot."

"That's about half hour away, miss."

"I know."

He eyed my dingy t-shirt and ripped jeans with a fresh dirt mark skeptically. "As long as you can pay," he stated in broken English, and stared at me in the review mirror. "We prosecute non-payers."

"Go," I said glaring at him.

We took off, passing the entrance of what was my home. It wasn't fancy or new, but it had been mine. The only real home I'd ever had, and I felt like I'd been hit in the gut with a baseball bat. I'd been hysterical too many times in the last few days, I wasn't going to cry anymore. I couldn't afford to. I had no one but myself, and no one wanted to rely on a hysterical woman, including me.

Chapter Nine

I hadn't meant to, but I'd fallen asleep waiting for my bus, as I sat on the ground alongside the building. In my hand was a ticket to L.A. It was a city with enough people to get lost, at least for now. The ticket was still firmly in my grasp as I awoke to a shoe nudging my side.

"Where are you going?"

I knew the voice instantly. Cormac. I cursed in my head. I looked up, and expected to see his men with him, but he was alone.

"How much do you weigh?"

He looked taken aback by the question but answered, "Two hundred and forty lbs."

Yep, no shot. "I think you just answered your own question."

He had the nerve to laugh. "Come on. We'll talk on the way back," he said.

It was still early enough that the bus depot was empty, and I weighed my options. I knew I couldn't take him, but would going with him willingly be the height of stupidity? Last time I'd followed one of them without a thought hadn't ended well.

"Don't make this difficult."

"Why, so you can try to kill me in the privacy of your own home? Why not just do it here?"

He squatted down, eye level with me. "If I wanted you dead, you would be. I never wanted to hurt you. I thought I had no choice. Now that I do, I have no intention of killing you."

"What about the repercussions you talked about?"

"You didn't go far enough for them to apply."

I knew he was being honest with me, but my body rebelled as I sat frozen.

"I understand why you don't trust me. I'd have to be an imbecile not to. But you have my word that I'm not going to physically harm you."

He held out his hand to me, as a symbol of his word. I stared at it for a moment, leaving it to hover between us for a good half a minute. Half a minute might not seem like a long time in the everyday scheme of things, but when you're talking about a full thirty seconds of awkwardness and possible rejection, it seems like forever.

He smiled as I took his hand finally, and again, that strange fission of energy seeped into my skin where we touched. I wanted to pull back from him, not because the connection felt bad, but because it felt strong. I didn't want to feel any kind of connection to him.

He looked down at our still joined hands, and I realized he felt it, too. His mask slipped just enough that I could see that it disarmed him as well. Even so, he held my hand all the way to the car until I became self-conscious. I didn't want to break the connection first and show any unease or weakness, but I was afraid the clamminess of my hands would reveal me, anyway.

He finally released my hand when he opened the door to a jet-black sports car. I climbed into the seat made from the softest leather I'd ever felt.

"What kind of car is this?" I asked, as he got into the driver's seat.

"It's an Aston Martin."

"It's pretty."

"Thanks," he said, and his lips twitched upward.

"Do I amuse you?" I asked, as I bristled. My life was being turned upside down, and this guy thought everything I said was funny.

"Don't do that."

"Do what?"

"Get all defensive. It's not a bad thing."

I turned my gaze back toward the road and let it drop. I had bigger fish to fry, things more important than whether or not I amused him. "So, let's talk," I said looking to get to the heart of the matter.

"Are you hungry?"

"I wasn't referring to small talk."

"What's wrong with small talk?"

"I don't like it."

"It's probably because you aren't very good at

it, are you?"

"That has nothing to do with it."

"That's why it bothers you."

"No, I'm not good at it. You are?"

"I'm not a huge fan, but I can hold my own."

"Can we talk about more serious matters, now?"

"If you insist, but it probably won't be good."

"Why not?"

"I'm not sure if you are aware of this, but you get a bit irritable on more sensitive subjects."

In spite of myself I laughed. I knew I was rough around the edges but I wasn't used to people besides Lacey pointing it out.

"So why did you try to leave?" he asked.

My gut told me he already knew the answer. He had found me within hours of my departure, which confirmed he was having me watched, no surprise there. He was testing me again. Everything with this man was a test.

"Vitor came to see me, but you know that, so, clearly I'm not going to lie about it. If you want to play games, find someone else. I don't like them."

He hopped on the highway and let the engine loose. The speed shot a huge surge of adrenaline through me, as if I didn't have enough flooding my system already.

"What did he say?" His voice was calm, but I heard something in his tone I couldn't quite identify.

"He wanted to talk. He wanted to tell me a little bit about himself. Now I have a couple of questions. Only fair I think."

"Shoot."

"Vitor isn't human?"

"Nope."

"And you are the one who helps them *get around* so to speak? But we are human right?"

"Yes."

"Why don't you want to help him?"

"What I feel about the situation doesn't matter. It's not my choice whether or not to allow them to move to Earth. I don't own this planet. But, I do have to add, regardless of what he says, they've already destroyed their world. That doesn't give me a real warm fuzzy feeling about asking them to move in, even if it were up to me."

"He said they have technology that could help."

"He says a lot of things. Do you want to let them all come on over?"

"He said people are gathering to move against you?"

"Yep, that sounds about right."

"When does this deal end? I don't remember reading about war activities in the small print on that contract I signed." And when can I get the hell away from this mess. I thought my life was messed up before? This put things in perspective.

"Not sure," he replied with a shrug of his shoulders.

"Yes, well, that doesn't really work for me."

"I'm not trying to play with you. There are a lot of factors at work."

"Which leads to my next question, what are we exactly? This seems a bit beyond making some pocket change and good skin."

"I'll tell you whatever you want to know, but you do understand there's no going back?" He turned toward me to make sure I understood him. "You have a couple of drinks one night and slip, no one is going to let you off the hook."

"Didn't we already establish the whole secrecy thing? *I get it.* Now look at the road if you don't mind, and start spilling."

"I'll do better than tell you."

I felt a jolt in the road and realized it was one of the Lacard driveway speed bumps. We fell quiet as he pulled over to the curb. The moment we came to a full stop the valet took his car.

"Take that to my suite," he said to the valet, and I turned to see my duffle bag disappear. Oh shit, that didn't bode well for my evening. He could have had the valet check it for me to pick up later, but he didn't.

We walked to his elevator in silence, and I noticed more than a few pairs of eyes watch us cross the casino floor, including Vicky's. I knew what it looked like, but I'd stopped caring about what people thought of me years ago. If they wanted to imagine me sleeping with the boss, let them. That was a lot easier pill to swallow than what I'd grown up with. They meant nothing to me.

When we stepped into his elevator, I thought we would head up but we dropped instead, and I had to remind myself that I had his word on my safety. Did I believe him? Yes. If he still wanted to kill me, like he said, I'd probably already be dead. Hell, any one of them could've killed me in my trailer. No one would have noticed me for days.

When the elevator opened, we stepped into a small square hallway. As the doors closed behind us, a panel opened revealing a keyboard. He dialed in a code, then a beam of light scanned his iris and the second set of doors opened. I followed him into a long hallway that had to be at least a mile long.

"I didn't realize the casino was so big."

"This area is larger, but it's close."

"When do we get to the whole top secret area?" I tried to sound glib, but I wasn't sure I'd pulled it off.

He stopped suddenly in front of one of many doors. "Now." He opened a door and waited for me to enter.

I heard him shut it, as I looked around. The room was the size of my high school gymnasium, but its walls, ceilings, and floors, were the polished dull grey of a pencil tip. A line of computers and equipment lined the back wall and there were two enormous monoliths of polished ebony at the opposite side of the room.

Drawn to them, I walked over to the closest one and ran my fingers along the veins that ran through the stone. When I touched them, I imagined I could feel a pulse running through them. It felt so real I drew my hand back quickly.

"What are they?" I asked in awe.

"These help us to open a portal. This is where we transport."

I pulled my eyes from their beauty to see him standing a few feet behind me, admiring them as well. He walked forward and stopped next to me. I watched him graze the ebony surface with his fingers, like I had done, tracing the pattern across its sleek surface. An image of him grazing his fingers across my skin popped into my head. He turned his face to me and I swear he could read my thoughts. His eyes were intense as they stared at my face and lingered a second too long on my lips.

He turned his back to the monolith and leaned against it with a knowing smirk.

"Don't look at me like that. There isn't a chance in hell." I took a couple of steps to gain some distance. "Now, explain this to me?" I turned my back to him and looked around the room.

"Come here." He pushed off and walked toward a desk where a small dark stone lay. It looked like the same material as the larger monoliths but a fraction of the size. He picked it up and tossed it to me.

I held it warily, not wanting to close my hand around it. I held it far from my body with my palm open.

"Close your hand around it."

"Why?" I asked, as I stalled.

"The way you are acting, I think you already know."

"I have no idea what you are talking about."

"Then do it."

"No, it's stupid," I said, and tried to blow him off. I had the feeling that Cormac wasn't put off his track that easily.

He walked toward me and went to touch my fingers, but I pulled away before he could.

"Fine." I closed my hand, and felt the cold stone warm in my hand, then tingle. I prayed for nothing to happen. Sometimes it wouldn't, but a bad feeling made me think this wasn't one of those times.

"Open your hand."

I hesitated, feeling the pressure and afraid to release it, afraid to confirm what he already knew, what I'd spent years of my life hiding. I knew that he expected what was going to happen. He was the same thing, whatever an alchemist actually was, but old habits do really die hard. After hiding something for so long, I couldn't seem to get my fingers to relax their grip.

"It's okay," he said, as he stepped forward and pried my fingers open.

The stone shot through the air like a bullet and buried itself into the lead ceiling above.

"Well, that's interesting," Cormac said, as he stared at the ceiling in interest.

"What do you mean? I thought you knew what was going to happen."

"It's much stronger than I would have imagined. I should have guessed it would be after how quickly your body shot out those bullets, but Buzz isn't the best shot. I thought he might have grazed you with some of them."

The mental calculation he was making showed openly on his face. What I'd done truly surprised him.

"Care to clue me in?"

"You're a half breed. I don't understand how it's this strong. Only full bloods usually have this much strength." He was still staring at the ceiling. His emotionless mask back in place, so I could no longer read his thoughts. "This is interesting," he added, but I guessed he was talking more to himself than me.

"Half breed?"

"Alchemists, or that's how we started out thousands of years ago, before we evolved into what we are now. Now we are mostly called Keeprs." He watched me now and waited for this to sink in.

"You turn metal into gold and something about the fountain of youth?" That was the beginning and end of what I knew about alchemy and all I remembered from surfing Google.

"That was one of the original goals, but we surpassed that a long, long, time ago. What you just did was change that stone into exotic matter."

My brain scrambled as I remembered that term from a science class. "Doesn't that have something to do with wormholes?"

"It has everything to do with wormholes. A wormhole is a shortcut to a different place in the galaxy, sometimes a different universe. Wormholes normally aren't traversable for two reasons, they collapse under the gravity generated by the space time fabric, and they emit huge amounts of radiation. If you didn't get crushed, you die from the nastiest sunburn you've ever seen." He motioned toward the stone still stuck in the ceiling. "Exotic matter counteracts the gravity."

"And the radiation?"

"It isn't poisonous to Keepers. We can draw

the radiation omitted to us like a vacuum, and we are immune to it. We simply absorb it like a sponge would sop up water. Then our bodies use the energy, similar to someone else digesting a steak dinner."

"And that's what I've been doing, turning things into exotic matter. How do I hurt people?"

"Yeah, that's a cute trick you do. I haven't seen anyone use our ability in that way for a long time. That's why I didn't recognize it when you used it on Tracker in the casino. How did you start doing that?"

"I don't know," I said vaguely, not wanting to give him the desperate details of the first time it had happened.

He waited for a moment, but then let it go and continued. "You're exciting their cells."

"I don't understand what you mean?"

"You are stimulating them into a frenzy, which applies pressure to the surrounding areas as well. I'd imagine it would be extremely painful. You could burst bones if you did it strongly enough."

"But I thought alchemists did things with chemicals? They didn't change things with their bodies and minds. How can that be done by touch alone?"

"Once our ancestors learned how to distort different object's physical natures, and how to create exotic matter, we were able to create a stable wormhole. Some of the portals that opened led to nothing but barren lands, or just space. But some of the portals led to a planet with humanoid races. Once we learned how to communicate with them, we discovered they had their own unique skill set. Where humans have a conscious brain and a subconscious, their brains are a single united process. Certain functions remain on autopilot, but they can override anything in their systems. They can consciously alter their brain patterns. In exchange for passage through the wormhole, they helped meld our skills into our subconscious."

"I don't get it."

"We consciously control our energy and the energy around us. Matter on a very small scale is vibrations. Different vibrations change what the matter is. We simply change the vibrations."

"And that is how I healed?"

"No, you healed because of your subconscious skills, although we aren't as adept as they are at it. Their brains are a single consciousness. Our subconscious has some reasoning abilities, but it can't communicate freely with our conscious. Your brain knew you were about to be shot, so your cells simply were prepared. They concentrated in the outer parts of your head to limit entrance and then forced the bullets out."

"But once I was shot, how would my brain keep doing that if I'm passed out?"

"Your brain doesn't stop working, your conscious brain just isn't aware of it. When your alarm clock goes off, your subconscious wakes you. It's always aware of what's around."

"You know that sounds insane, right?"

He pointed upward toward the stone still lodged in the ceiling above us. "But that's normal? With the bullets, it was simply a matter of changing your body's density temporarily."

I wasn't completely shocked. How could I be? I'd lived my whole life knowing things weren't the way people believed. I'd gotten shot in the head and walked away. That didn't mean I was at ease with this reality, either. I now had confirmed proof, and thinking something and knowing something can be worlds apart. I leaned a hip on the table he had taken the stone from, as I tried to act as if I was taking this in stride, even though my insides felt like a churning mass of mush.

"I saw that man, Tracker, change. What was he?"

"For lack of a more sophisticated term, you would know him as a werewolf."

"And this alien werewolf person, he is one of the races that helped merge your abilities?"

"No, Tracker isn't that skilled. He and his kind are on the lower rungs of their civilization. Vitor's race, also known as Fae here on earth, are the kind that helped us. In essence, Tracker's race just came along for the ride."

"And who are these people gathering against you that Vitor warned of?"

"Vitor himself."

"Why would he warn me about him?"

"He's playing you."

"And how do I know anything you say is true?"

"You don't."

"Why did you shoot me that night? Because of this?" I waived my hand to encompass everything in the room.

"We thought you were a human. There is a binding agreement between our races that all human witnesses are eliminated. When you saw Tracker change that night, you were in a private area of the casino, a safe zone. Your life was forfeit. If we didn't kill you, he'd have tracked you down and done it himself. A quick death at our hand was a kindness."

A shiver passed through me. "Spare me your kindness in the future. I'd rather take my chances."

He ignored my sarcasm and continued. "Once your body forced the bullets out, we knew you were one of us. Now that we know what you are, it's different. You're a Keeper, and as such, you fall under my domain. They would have to get clearance from me to touch you."

"And who keeps me safe from you?" I nailed him with the frostiest stare I had. He talked to me and explained things as if we were on good terms, but I wouldn't be lulled by his relaxed demeanor. "You didn't think bygones would be bygones after you had me shot in the head five times, did you? We'd start singing Kumbaya?"

He shrugged his shoulders and walked across the room and I found myself admiring his grace as he moved. I was annoyed at myself. If my subconscious supposedly had some reasoning ability of its own, it was a real masochist. I thought hard, trying to send it the message that it was a complete idiot. He was the enemy. You don't find the enemy attractive, it didn't matter how hot he was, you moron.

"I get that you're pissed, but I had to do it. Now I don't."

"And when that changes?"

"It won't."

"Great. That's very reassuring. Cause things never change in life, right?"

"Why did you try to run?"

"Why wouldn't I? I've no desire to get messed up in whatever you have going on."

"It's a little late for that. This day's been coming since the day you were born. For a half-breed, you have way too much power flowing through your veins. Strolling around, untrained as you are, it was only a matter of time before you started to cause a problem for us. I can't fathom

97

how you managed to avoid detection for this long."

"I've managed. When freaky stuff starts happening around you all the time, you'd be amazed at how easy it is to remain alone." I didn't add how lonely I'd been, but I'd gotten by. People had much worse lives then I had. I wasn't going to cry in my sleep over being alone.

He was watching me with all too knowing eyes, and I didn't like the pity I thought I read in them.

"Stop," I snapped.

"I'm sorry."

"You don't need to pity me, you're the murderer," I accused him, trying anything to shut down the entire exchange that was hitting me way too hard. I looked at him, hoping to see anger. Even violence was preferable to this. I could handle anger and violence. I was used to those things. "Are you letting me leave or not?" My voice was starting to rise. I never raised my voice. It declared how upset you were, a satisfaction I didn't like to give to anyone.

He reached down on the table near me, toying with a few papers and I jumped up and moved across the room.

"I was hoping to give you a little time to acclimate, bring you into the fold slowly, but it's not working out like that."

"So what does that mean?"

"It means that I need you to be on the grounds here at the casino full time. You can still go wherever you choose, but you'll need to take an escort."

"No, absolutely not."

"I don't have a choice. Vitor, and whoever else is involved, is determined to destroy the portal. It's bad now. If they were to get their hands on you, it could be much worse. I'm trying to make this as easy for you as I can."

"So what if they took me? What if they took you or one of your guys?"

"Not all my men are Keepers. The ones who are, they wouldn't be able to take alive."

"So we can die?"

"Yes."

"What if I were trained?"

"You'd have to swear loyalty to me. Are you ready to do that?"

"Sure!" I said with the most enthusiasm I could muster. All this, without ever taking a single acting class. I thought I sounded pretty believable.

He laughed and walked closer to me. "It would have to be sincere."

"How about you train me, and we'll see how the loyalty thing works out?"

"I can't turn you into a weapon that could be used against me."

"So then, what? I live in your casino

indefinitely?"

I watched him closely, and saw his façade cracking just slightly to reveal what looked like uncertainty. "I don't know," he said finally. We'd hit a stalemate.

As we left the room, we fell into silence as I followed him back upstairs. My mind ran wild thinking of the implications. Alternate universes were straight out of my scifi shows, and knowing that perhaps I could control the opening to such a thing made me heady with possibilities. Having that power was almost enough to make me want to swear loyalty. But not quite.

As we stood in the elevator together, I knew we were heading to his penthouse, and I remembered I had a shift tonight.

"I need to go get a few things from my place. I need my uniform for tonight. Lucky for me, my job is in the casino. Maybe my goons can just blend in with the regular ol' casino goons." I said this with fake optimism.

"You do realize that an alchemist can change base metals into gold. If you swore allegiance, you'd never have to work another day in your life." He looked at me with eyebrows raised.

I stared at the walls and crossed my arms over my chest. I hated being alone in close quarters with him. He smelled too good, he looked too good and it was just completely unfair. Villains were supposed to be ugly. Just another way I was getting screwed in this deal. My villain didn't even look like he was supposed to. "I'm sure I'd just get bored."

"There are also other ways to be entertained." The look on Cormac's face left little doubt as to what he was referring.

"From what I've heard, you've got enough entertaining to do."

"I can always make time."

"I wouldn't want to impose. I'll just stick to the waitressing for now so I don't clutter up your schedule."

He looked back at the elevator doors and sighed. "If that's what you prefer, but you don't know what you're missing out on."

We walked down his long hallway and I admired the paintings, like I did every time I saw them. If nothing else, I was starting to like the hallway.

We stepped in as Ben held the door.

"Ben, our little porcupine here will be staying in the spare bedroom."

"I've already put the contents of her bag away."

I said thank you, but I was annoyed someone had gone through my personal belongings. I puttered around my new suite of rooms for a while, digging through the closet and the drawers finding all of my things. I was sure Ben made a good salary, so it was ridiculous to think he'd take some of my things, plus what would a middle aged man do with my stuff, anyway? But having to fight for years and years to keep anything had ingrained a distrust in me that didn't easily let go. Even as I fought the feelings with logic, I still had to locate every last item.

I found my book of Monet prints still in my knapsack. I guess he hadn't been sure what to do with that as it looked out of place here with its binding held together with duck tape. I knew it was foolish to pack it, but I couldn't seem to leave it behind.

I'd just finished counting my bras, Ben could turn out to be a pervert after all, when Cormac called me into the foyer to tell me lunch was coming up. Ben had left to go get us food from the casino kitchens, so it was just me and Cormac in the room and it felt beyond awkward.

I was just about to make some excuse that I hadn't thought of yet, to go back in my room, when Dodd barged in. He paused inside the door breathing heavily, his eyes looking frantic.

"What is it?" Cormac asked immediately.

Dodd's eyes darted to me for a second, then back to Cormac. "We have a problem."

"How bad?"

Dodd didn't speak, just shook his head.

"Come on," Cormac said, as he walked out the

door and Dodd followed him immediately. I stood watching them leave and wondered what had happened to make Dodd look so bad. These weren't the type of men that became rattled. "Come on!" Cormac said again, and looked straight at me.

"A simple please would suffice."

He rolled his eyes and didn't say please, but I went with them, anyway. As much as I wanted to be left alone I didn't mind going with them. I wanted to see what would affect them this much.

I followed quickly behind, glad that I was a runner and could keep up with their larger frames. We climbed into the private elevator, and plummeted an unknown number of floors, until I found myself in the hallways we had just left not more than a couple hours before. But, where the area had felt abandoned then, now it bustled with people. They all gave Cormac a wide berth, and a few threw a passing glance at my presence, but no one spoke a word. I wouldn't have either, with the energy Cormac was throwing off.

He stormed into the room with the portal, and as I entered behind him, I saw a crowd in the center. Everyone was gathered around something I couldn't see, but they parted quickly as Cormac approached.

Once I saw, I wished I hadn't. A man was lying in the center, his clothes in tatters and his flesh

103

was raw. On the skin that was bare, blisters oozed and wept. Any area that wasn't blistered was a raw and angry red. He didn't appear to be conscious, and I was glad. The pain would've been unbearable.

Cormac kneeled by the man's side. "What happened?" Cormac barked into the room. No one spoke, and the room became deathly quiet. I realized people weren't even moving, afraid to draw attention to themselves. "What happened!" Cormac repeated as he stood to his full height.

A young, small, brunette stepped forward. "We don't know sir. We had started everything as planned, all seemed to be going well. We didn't know anything was wrong until he stepped out."

"Who was on point?" Cormac asked.

A blond man in his thirties raised his hand.

"Kever, do you have any idea what went wrong?"

The man just shook his head. He looked close to tears.

"Were you taking in the radiation?"

"I was pulling at it, the same way I always do. I'm so sorry Cormac, I don't know what happened."

The man was clearly beyond distraught at what had happened, and I could physically see the aggression leaving Cormac as his limbs relaxed slightly. I, on the other hand, was glad we hadn't had our lunch yet. I found myself looking for a trash can nearby in case I got sick.

"Get him set up in a bed. Give him as much morphine as you need to keep him comfortable, if it's even possible. Dodd, call Tracker right away, tell him to get here. Send him up to me when he arrives." Cormac stormed out of the room.

Looking around the room, I decided to follow Cormac rather than stay here. The tension hung thick in the room, and I was better off waiting it out in my room, in solitude, while tempers calmed. Plus, I'd already seen more than I'd wanted.

I kept my distance, as I followed Cormac back. A fleeting thought ran through my head of trying another break out, but a quick glance at Cormac's stoic face, and still quite tense frame, made me think this wasn't the best time to push the issue. My confidence in making it out unseen had fallen to an all time low.

It wasn't until we walked into his penthouse that he finally spoke.

"Come into the living room for a minute. I would like to talk to you."

I paused. I didn't want to be near him right now with how volatile he seemed, and I tried to decide which way to turn; my new room, or follow him into the living room. I considered ignoring his request. I didn't owe him anything, he owed me.

"Please."

That word told me one thing. He was

105

desperate, really desperate. I walked into the living room. I could tell he was upset about the man but I wouldn't feel bad for him. I refused to. He wasn't my friend, ally or anything else. He was my enemy, or a nuisance if I felt like being generous. I followed him because, as I might have mentioned before, I don't like desperate people. They tend to do desperate things. Desperate people should be placated until you can get as far away from them as humanly possible, because desperate people had a bad tendency of blowing up and taking you with them.

I sat down on one of the now pristine matching couches, while he remained standing by the bar, and wondered if they kept spares in a warehouse somewhere. A quick glance showed the glass had also been repaired, not a scratch remained. It was as if the night had never happened, and it made me mad. As easily as that, nothing was left. If I had died that night, not even a stain would be there as proof of my slaughter.

"I need a favor."

I laughed, but it wasn't a laugh of joy. It told him, without words, what I thought of his request.

"I wouldn't ask if it was for me." He was a hair away from groveling. In theory, having this man grovel for anything should have appeased me, but in reality, it did nothing.

"And who is the favor for? Buzz? Dodd? Do

you think I would be willing to help them either?"

"I told you about the portal. What I didn't explain is why I need to keep control of it. Most involved view this as simply a business. I provide passage in and out of this universe for a price, but the reason is much larger. Only I and a select few know the entire truth. If I can't keep control of this operation, this entire world is in danger."

I snapped my head in his direction as I watched him go to the bar. The somber tone of his voice lent authenticity to what he said. He might be crazy or wrong, but he believed what he said. I watched him throw back the contents of an amber liquid I assumed to be scotch. He silently offered me a glass, which I declined, and he refilled his own.

"There are only a handful of portals. That is all that can exist at one time because of the distortions they create. We, the Keepers, are the only ones capable of controlling them. There have been defectors over the years, Keepers thirsting for more power who have joined with others. They've all been low level, none of them strong enough to open up and maintain another portal." He came and sat down across from me on the other couch, the one that had replaced the bloodied one. Even with this supposedly heavy burden hanging over his head, he was a striking looking man.

"What happens if others control a portal?

107

Why should you have all the power?" My question was argumentative and bordered on confrontational. I couldn't help myself, the more attractive I found him the more I felt compelled to fight against him. In truth it wasn't him I was fighting, it was my conscious brain, struggling with the workings of my subconscious desires that truly pissed me off right now. A subconscious that had a masochistic streak and wouldn't listen to reason.

"If someone like Vitor or Tracker gets control, there will be no end to the influx of other beings. One on one, they are much stronger than humans are and there will be no end of them in sight. Even if they don't rape this earth for all it has, they will be more powerful. It's only logical that they'll try a power grab. Right now, the only thing that keeps them in hiding is that if they were found out, they'd be so outnumbered they'd lose. Also, if this one has been opened recently, and another is opened too soon after, it creates turmoil in the space time fabric. This area could possibly explode."

"Possibly explode? Would it explode, or not?"

"It would all depend on how large a portal was opened, and how recently this one had closed. There are too many factors to predict accurately."

"Worst case scenario?" I asked. In my life, that's what I'd come to expect.

"The entire Vegas Strip could be destroyed."

"You've got to be kidding me!" I leaned my head back on the couch and rested my arm over my eyes.

"Afraid not."

"What do you want from me?" I asked, but I was afraid to hear the response.

"Today's incident isn't the first time something's gone wrong. Someone is messing with the portals, someone strong."

"So, go get Vitor and kick his ass. You don't need me."

"I would've if that was an option. I can't. Even if I was positive it was him, I need to know what Keepers are betraying me or it won't end. Someone else will step up and take over. There is at least one very strong Keeper involved in this, possibly more, and I need to take them out."

"Still don't see why you need me."

"I want to teach you how to control a portal and I need you to operate it with me."

"You've got other Keepers. Trained ones remember?"

"I already paired them up and I thought that would control it. As you just saw it didn't. You've got a lot of natural ability, and I can't take any more chances of being outgunned." Cormac's phone rang and interrupted our conversation, cutting off the reason why I was so important. "Thanks," he said then pressed the end button.

109

"Tracker is going to be here in two minutes. We've got to finish this later. The guy who got cooked in the portal was one of his men."

I got up without being asked and walked to my room, I had no desire to see Tracker, and try as I might, I wasn't cold enough to ignore such a loss.

Cormac followed me into the foyer, and then left through the main door. I waited about ten minutes, before I checked to see if anyone was in the hallway. There were two today. I sighed and went to go shower for my shift tonight. If I was going to be stuck here, I might as well earn some cash. I didn't plan on being stuck for long, and when I left, I was going to need the money.

Chapter Ten

"Let me through!"

"Not until Cormac says so," said one of the burly door guards.

"What's the matter?" I heard Cormac's voice before I saw him.

"My shift started five minutes ago. You said that I would be able to come and go as I please, but I guess not," I said accusingly and waited for his reaction.

"Let her through," he said to them. The moment they moved to the side, I headed down the hallway toward the elevator that would take me to the casino. I'd almost been out of earshot when I heard him tell them, "But keep your eye on her from a distance."

I wasn't surprised at all. I'd expected it. I would play by his rules for a while. Maybe even agree to help, while I learned how to control this thing I could do.

I put it to the back of my mind, as I got to the high rollers section where I waitressed. I saw Lacey leaning on the bar laughing at something Jonny said.

"Where have you been? You missed class," she said as soon as I came to stand next to her.

"Hi, beautiful."

"Hi, Jonny. I was really sick. I think it might have been food poisoning."

"That's the worst!" Lacey responded and Jonny cringed. The moment Jonny walked to the other end of the bar, Lacey leaned in close to me. "I heard you came back with Cormac? What's the deal? Did you hook up with him?"

"No!" My face scowled when I said it.

"Really? Everyone here heard about you walking in with him at the crack of dawn, well, everyone but Jonny." She nodded her head in his direction. "I don't think anyone wants to tell him." She finished with a little giggle.

"Shut up," I said quickly, as Jonny walked back over to us.

"Jo, don't look, but that creep that was bothering you the other night is back," Jonny said.

"Where?"

"He's in my section." Lacey offered. "I heard about that too. They shouldn't even let him back in the place." She shook her head in indignation.

I looked over and saw the man named Tracker at a black jack table and my skin crawled. All I could see was fur and a large muzzle with pointy teeth now. It had been gruesome. Cormac said that he would have killed me violently if given the chance. Looking at him, I believed it. I had gotten the worst kind of vibe off him the night I had met him, but I had to let it go and just get to work. It would paralyze me with fear if I didn't.

Once I got into the swing of things, it was strange how the routine made me feel a little bit normal, even with everything else going on. The casino was packed, and so I had been going nonstop since shortly after I started. I saw some of Cormac's door thugs lingering here and there, but they blended into the background and kept their distance.

I'd been so busy, I'd barely noticed when Tracker got up and went to leave, but I caught the movement of the garish candy apple red leather jacket he was wearing as it moved across the room. I was relieved he was leaving, as I watched him cross the floor, wanting to confirm the moment he was gone.

"I hear you moved into Cormac's?"

I rolled my eyes before I turned to face Vicky. Right now, it was just a rumor of me being with him. If she knew I was staying there, it was only a matter of time before the whole casino knew.

"Where I'm staying is none of your business."

"You're a whore. He's just using you because you're easy, so enjoy it while it lasts, because he'll get bored and throw you away like the trash you are."

"Get out of my face," I said. She was in my personal space. That was almost as bad as touching me, in my book. "Or I'll move you."

"You think you can?" she sneered.

Vicky had pure ghetto running through her veins, but she was too stupid to have learned how to tone it down, like I did. She was also too stupid to recognize that I wasn't a stranger to the streets myself.

I pulled myself to my full height, just a few inches shy of Vicky's, and instead of holding back, I let every ounce of my own harsh upbringing show through. The nice, innocent, girl-next-door façade I usually wore slid from my features like butter across a warm skillet. I could see the shock on her face before I even uttered a word.

"You don't know who you're messing with. Back off before I lose my patience and drag your skinny ass out of here, then beat you to within an inch of your life."

"You're a sicko," she said, but then she walked a little too quickly back to the bar and the safety of others.

"Very nice." It was Cormac's voice from behind me. I was annoyed on so many levels. First off, I was tired of people sneaking up behind me. It showed how off my game I was. Second, I wanted to cringe at what he had just witnessed. I didn't like anyone to see that side of me. The side I had developed out of desperation from being a young girl in a mean world and having no one else to depend on.

Just then, a group of women walked past to the left which only highlighted the differences. They wore heels and had pretty hair and nails. They laughed over something that was probably light and frivolous. They were soft and feminine, everything I wasn't. I could fake it all day long, but I'd never truly be one of them. That was what men wanted, not someone like me. I felt jaded and dirty compared to them.

I didn't care though. This man was my enemy. Why should I care what he thought of me?

He walked up and stood next to me, close enough that I could feel the heat of his body. I could see him stare at me, out of the corner of my eye, but I busied myself looking down at my order pad instead of meeting his gaze.

He leaned down close to my ear and said in the softest whisper, "Am I making you uncomfortable Jo?"

His warm breath on my ear sent a shiver down my spine. I wanted to instantly take a step away, but that would be almost as bad as admitting it, so I held my ground and forced myself to meet his eyes. "No, why would you?"

"That's good. I wouldn't want to make you nervous." He ran a finger along the length of my arm. "Are you cold?"

"A little," I lied, knowing he had noticed the goose bumps on my skin.

115

He smiled down at me. He had a beautiful smile, dimples and all. "We're going to be spending a lot of time together," he said. "I really do want you to feel comfortable." His hand came to rest on the small of my back.

"Maybe it's better if we aren't too comfortable, considering that you are my boss."

He laughed. "Why? Do you feel sexually harassed?"

"No."

"Then I guess I'll have to try harder next time."

My heart was beating out of my chest as he walked away.

Chapter Eleven

Cormac, true to his word, had given me free rein. I always had a shadow, but my movements hadn't been restricted in the least. He had also disappeared. I wasn't sure where he went, but I hadn't seen him in almost a week.

I tried to go back to school, but when I did, I was called down to the Dean's office. When I got there, I was told I was being given special permission to finish all my classes, including my finals, via email. It seemed Cormac's influence extended pretty far. I told him it was unnecessary, but the Dean insisted.

Other than my waitress shifts, I had nothing left to do but hang around the apartment while I researched alchemy. The first couple of days I stayed mostly in my room on my laptop, but then as no one seemed to be around, I started to venture out more and more. I was starting to wonder if he actually even lived there. Maybe it was a front? Maybe he didn't want people to know where he really lived. I hadn't even seen Ben, the door-guy-butler or whatever he was.

I'd just finished showering. I hated getting dressed right after showering. My clothes always stuck to my still damp skin. So, I lounged in my room wearing the nicest black lace push up bra and matching underwear I'd ever owned.

A day or so after Cormac left me, one of the thugs by the door handed me a note. In it, he told me I had been provided with an account, and I could pick up anything I needed in Lacard's mall since he knew I only had what I had jammed into a knapsack, and he asked that I not venture back to my trailer until he returned. I had tried to stay on the conservative side at first, and then remembered that the guy had ordered me shot. That's when my shopping spree had turned ugly, or awesome, depending on your viewpoint. It's why I was now strutting around in lingerie that would make a Victoria Secret model jealous.

If I hadn't gone shopping, I would have been in grandma type underwear and a sports bra. If I hadn't gone shopping, Cormac might not have been staring at me like he was now. I had the stereo so loud I didn't hear him come in. Wound up for days, I'd decided to grab a wine glass and a bottle of wine from the bar. So there I was; perusing wines with my breasts practically grazing my chin. The tiniest swatch of lace with some small ribbon-like strands, were serving as underwear.

He cleared his throat, and that was when I finally realized he was there. I wasn't sure how long he had been standing there and my mind raced back over the last few moments and the poses I had probably presented him. I've never been one to blush, and I didn't then, either, but I was as close to it as I had ever been in my life.

I went to rush out of the room and that's when I looked in his eyes and saw the heat there. I'd seen it before, but I hadn't realized how much he had held back. My knees went weak, and I got a lump in my throat. There was no denying it anymore. Of all the men I'd met, I'd never been this sexually attracted to any of them. And it had to be this man? It didn't matter how I felt. I'd never let this happen. Ever. He stood still in his spot in the doorway, as I squeezed around him trying to avoid all contact and ran from the room.

I didn't leave my room again. I tossed and turned all night, and when I finally fell asleep, I dreamt of him. I dreamt of all the things I would never do.

When I finally poked my head out in the morning, he was there sitting on the couch with a room service table in front of him, eating breakfast.

"I ordered you pancakes," he said, not bothering to look up.

"Any coffee?"

"Full pot of hazelnut."

And just like that, we silently agreed to ignore last night. But something had changed. I wasn't sure I'd be able to describe this difference if I had to, but it hovered, like an electrical charge in the air before a lightning strike. There had been flirtation before, but it had seemed slightly playful, now it felt dangerous.

"You ready to finish our conversation from the other day?"

"Sure." I was more agreeable than normal, as I clung to anything that was nonsexual in nature.

"I had started to tell you, I need your help."

"But you didn't tell me why you needed me in particular."

"Keepers are born with different levels of power."

I nodded my head for him to continue, as I sat across from him and settled a plate of pancakes on my lap.

"We can't all alter physics. Some of us can't do it at all, some to a small degree. Each individual's capabilities are hindered or enhanced by the abilities they are born with."

He placed a steaming cup of coffee on the table next to me. I loved the smell of coffee in the morning.

"I don't get it. If you can alter physics, why can't you just alter *their* physics so they can do it?" I asked while I watched him over the rim of my porcelain cup.

"It's a part of our brain that controls it. The brain can be very tricky. Several generations ago, several Keepers dabbled in trying to amp up people's abilities."

"And?"

"It didn't go so hot. I've met a couple of the people who volunteered for the experiment. They aren't quite all there anymore."

My mouth formed a silent O, and he just nodded in agreement.

"You still haven't explained how I'm going to help you."

I put my plate of pancakes down on the side table and tucked my legs up underneath me. He sat forward on the couch, already dressed in his standard black slacks and crisp white shirt. His sleeves always rolled up, baring his corded forearms, and the button at his neck was always undone. It was as if he tried to don the outfit he felt he should wear, or perhaps the one society expected to see, but found it too constrictive for what he really was.

"You are uncommonly strong. What happened the other night, when the portal went wrong, it wasn't the first time. It has happened to me as well. Something, or someone, is blocking our absorption of the radiation."

"And you can't fix it?"

He leaned forward, resting his arms on his legs. "No. Meanwhile, we need to open the portal at least once a day. This is what prevents other portals from opening. The shorter the time frame

121

between openings, the stronger the Keeper needs to be to open one anywhere else."

"Why can't you just stop transporting people?"

"If we won't transfer people in and out, it will get very ugly, very quickly. It might even start a war. One I can't take the chance of losing. Like I said before, a lot of things hinge on keeping things running smoothly. It's also a matter of image. The weaker I seem; the more people will join against me. I don't know how many Keepers they have now, but I can't risk losing any more to them. I need to not show any vulnerability."

"So, now you want my help?"

"You're not just helping me."

"Yes, helping to clean up a mess that your people and your men started. These wormholes were nothing before your people. Now you guys screw it up, and I'm supposed to run right in and be thrilled to help you?"

"I think you are forgetting that the people who started this whole mess are your people too?"

Shit. He had a point. "Okay, maybe you're right. But the way I see it, I've got no motivation to help right now. I help you clean up this mess and I'm stuck. I don't help and I'm still stuck."

He pushed his sleeves up a little farther on his arms. His biceps straining beneath a refinement that didn't quite fit what I sensed was truly there.

"I'll make it worth your while. Whatever you want?"

"Let's see, hmmmm, maybe getting my life back would be a good start. Perhaps, even make me want to be cooperative?"

"You know that's the one thing I can't do." He leaned his head down and ran his fingers through his hair in frustration. "Anything else, money, cars, whatever."

I looked away from him, and took the few steps to the window. I stared at the Vegas horizon, as I liked to do. The Luxor's black pyramid was one of my favorite sights, the lights glowing along its edges. "I want to know when you plan to let me leave, and…" I hesitated finishing. I hated revealing anything that showed softness, but this mattered to me. Deep down, no matter how jaded I had become, or what I said, I would do whatever I could to help avert the disaster that might be coming. I might as well get something I wanted. "I want to know who my parents are."

As soon as the words left my mouth, I did something that I hadn't done since a small child. I blushed.

"Deal. But I can't guarantee anything."

There was an odd tone in his voice. I took a deep breath and looked over at him. "Stop looking at me like that!"

"Like what?" he asked.

"Like I'm some lost puppy you need to help. Just because I'm curious doesn't mean I'm soft." I walked toward my room.

"It's okay to want to know your parents. We aren't meant to be alone." His voice indicated he was right behind me, following me as I walked.

"You have no idea why I want to know." I got to the threshold of my bedroom door and turned to block him. "Don't start thinking I'm some little girl that is all soft in the center and needs some man to save her."

He was leaning on the wall outside my room. He looked at me, and then slowly smiled. "I think deep down, underneath all that blustering, you're as soft as a kitten." His hand reached out and toyed with a lock of my long hair, then let it drop.

I couldn't think of a single witty comeback, so I cursed him and slammed the door in his face. I could hear the bastard laughing through the door.

"We start tomorrow," I heard him call out before his footsteps retreated.

Chapter Twelve

"Where's Cormac?"

I turned to see Dodd stroll in the living room. "How would I know?"

"What are you eating?"

"What's it look like? What do you want?" As much as I would like to complain about everything, there were a couple of perks to staying here that I couldn't deny. The menu was insane. They'd make me whatever I wanted to eat, no matter what time I called it in. The turkey club sandwich I was eating right now was among my favorites. How could you go wrong with something that had bacon and mayo?

Before I knew what he was doing, Dodd's fingers swooped in and stole a quarter of my club sandwich.

"Hey! Go get your own food!" If Dodd hadn't been one of the men on the night of my almost murder, I would have offered him some.

"There's no way you were going to finish that, it's huge," he said in between bites. Then he had the audacity to reach in and grab some fries.

"You're missing the point. We," I pointed to him and then back to me, "are not friends." I shook my head emphasizing my point. "You do not get any of my french fries because of that."

"What are we watching?" He plopped down on the couch across from me and kicked off his shoes. "What is this crap?" he asked, as he looked at the TV.

"I like 'this crap'. You don't need to watch it. You can leave."

"Gimme the remote."

"No."

"So, I heard you're going to start training?"

"Why do you keep talking to me?"

"Why wouldn't I?"

"Because of what you took part in? I would think you would realize what that means?"

"Yeah, but that was before. You're one of us, now."

"I'm not one of you." I'd always wanted to belong. What a joke of fate for these to be the people who would accept me.

"I know we started off rough, but you are one of us. Fight it all you want, you'll see." He fluffed up his couch pillow, threw it behind his head, and continued watching TV.

I watched him settle in, made an unattractive grunt, and forfeited the living room to him. I'd barely made it back to my room when I heard Cormac come in.

"You ready to get started?"

"Coming," I hollered into the hallway. It wasn't my first choice of words for him, but I swallowed those back in an effort to keep the peace for now.

Cormac was standing in the foyer looking as sexy as ever, as he turned to watch me. It was beyond annoying. My knees went a little weak, as his pale blue eyes stalked my movements across the marble floor.

"Be there in five minutes boss man!" yelled Dodd from the living room.

"Why is he coming?"

"He wanted to help," Cormac stated mimicking my inflection.

"Fine. I guess being around one murderer or two isn't that much of a difference."

"I'm not a murderer."

"Did you order my murder?"

"I told you, it was complicated."

I could hear the aggravation in his voice and I rejoiced in pressing his buttons. "You say tomayto, I say tomahto. Same thing, isn't it?"

"No. It isn't."

"Yes, it is."

"No, it…I'm not doing this with you."

"You already are."

"No, I'm not, I'm going to rise above this and I refuse to argue with you."

"As much as I'd like to debate how you really aren't rising above anything, I'd rather know if you found anything out?" Ever since I found out about my mother, bloody in the church, the urgency I felt to find the truth had kicked up another notch.

"I've started the process. I have my lab running your blood sample against our databases. As soon as they find out anything, they are to tell me right away."

I nodded, looked at the floor in disappointment, and I felt him lay his hand on my shoulder and start to run it down my upper arm in a comforting gesture that had the exact opposite effect on me, as I quickly stepped back out of reach. He didn't touch me again but he did step forward, not crowding me, but giving me a strange sort of comfort none the less.

"What's going on?" Dodd asked, as he joined us in the foyer.

"Nothing. Just waiting for you," Cormac answered.

"Why does it feel weird in here?"

"Come on, we have a lot of work to do. I want her to be ready to operate a portal with me by Festiva."

"What's Festiva?"

Dodd answered "Once every year, we open up the portal and allow more people than normal through to join in an anniversary celebration."

"Anniversary of the portal?"

"Yes. We are busier than normal the days before, bringing everyone over. If we don't have this squared away by then, it could be very ugly," Dodd continued as we left the penthouse.

"Is it a good idea to bring more over under the circumstances? I'm not a tactical mastermind of any sort, but wouldn't you want less here?"

"And give them the impression that we are concerned? Absolutely not." Dodd said.

I turned to Cormac to see if he had a better explanation.

Reading the question on my face, he responded, "Yes, that about sums it up."

I just shook my head in disbelief as we headed down toward the lair beneath Lacard. It was truly startling that this entire operation was happening underneath a casino.

"Why a casino? Why not in the desert where there is nobody?" I asked them as we rode the elevator down.

"We need the people," Cormac explained. "We need to hide the high energy levels that the portals throw off."

"Portals? You said more than one right?"

"Yes. There are more than one, but nothing nearby."

"So, the other portals, are they in casinos as well?" I mentally started to calculate all of the areas known for large casinos.

"No. There are other options. This was just the most convenient for this area."

"You don't want to tell me the other locations? Really Cormac, haven't you ever heard in for a penny, in for a pound?"

"Maybe you should think on that yourself? Or as they say in poker, you are already pot committed."

"What?"

"When you play poker, and you have a significant amount of your money in the pot, it gets very hard to walk away. You, whether you want to acknowledge it or not, are pot committed."

"Maybe so, but I'm also skilled at getting out of a bad situation and simply disappearing, as my records have already proven."

I looked at him now as he leaned against the elevator wall, and it was hard not to admire his presence. It was beyond the grace of his movements. He owned the space. People instinctively looked to him to lead, and not because he was the boss. He had an air about him that made others follow. I'd noticed it in the casino, the deference he commanded. All eyes were always on him the moment he stepped into a room.

I started to follow Dodd out of the elevator but Cormac's arm around my waist stopped me.

"Maybe you can disappear from some people, but they aren't me." He removed his arm and walked out the elevator. "Sometimes we use amusement parks as well," he said as if that little moment hadn't even happened.

I watched his graceful movements as we entered the hallways that were now empty again, and I wondered where all the people went when the portal wasn't up and running.

We passed the door that I knew led to the portal and he opened up a room a few doors down. There was a step down when we entered and it was bare except for a line of work boots along one side. The walls, ceiling, and floor were a dull grey lead like the portal room. Other than that, it was completely bare.

"So what do we do?"

"This is where we train. What size shoe do you wear?" Cormac asked.

"Seven."

Dodd's phone started buzzing. "I gotta go handle that thing we were talking about."

Cormac nodded and Dodd headed out.

"Here, put these on. Make sure you lace them up tightly."

"Why do I have to switch shoes?" I asked as I slipped out of my own sneakers.

"These are special. When you start messing around with gravitational pulls, these will hold you to the ground if you can't handle it."

"Oh. Aren't you putting on a pair?"

"I don't need them." He reached down, took my sneakers and put them into a cabinet built into the wall.

"Are they comfortable?"

I looked down and cringed at the ugly brown utilitarian boots. "Yes."

"Stand in a comfortable position."

"I am."

He flipped a switch on the wall and a slight humming sound started.

"What is that?"

"Try to move your feet."

I went to lift a foot, and realized I was glued to the floor.

"Cormac, I don't like this."

The cloying feeling of claustrophobia was starting to suffocate me. I bent down, and started to take the boots off and he knelt next to me.

"You're not stuck. You can undo the laces at any point. But, once we start practicing, you might want them on so you don't end up on the ceiling."

I stopped what I was doing, and realized he was right. It wasn't like I couldn't take them off at any point. I nodded and stood up again.

Once I had calmed down, he walked to another built in cabinet and tossed four plastic children's balls into the room, the type that I always saw, but never got, in bins at the grocery stores growing up.

"Okay, I know you can convert single small items at a time. I need you to try to do these balls all at once, without touching them."

"But I can't reach them."

"I know. You have to do it without touching."

"I don't know how."

"It's the same way you did the stone. You don't need to touch them. Just let the energy flow through your hands. You can convert anything in your immediate area."

I held out my hands and tried to focus on letting some unseen energy flow through my fingers. Nothing happened.

"Remember when you attacked Tracker in the bar?"

"Of course I do."

"You did something extra, didn't you?"

I just smiled.

"Try pulling from the same place. It's all related."

I held out my hands again, and pulled from that place. I could feel the familiar tingle, but the balls didn't budge.

"I don't get it. I can feel it. Why doesn't it do what it's supposed to."

"I'm not sure. Usually we just do some fine tuning with control. I've never had to start from scratch. It's just something that happens. With you, I think you've trained your body to hold back for so long, that you have a hard time releasing beyond your immediate touch. Just keep trying, you'll get

133

it."

Two hours later, Cormac was sitting on the floor, holding up the wall and playing with his cell phone. I was squatted down on the floor, very uncomfortably I might add, with my boots frozen to the floor.

I gave up and completely lay down on the floor, knees still bent to accommodate the funny boots, and banged my head against the lead floor, staring at the ceiling.

"This isn't working. I think it's time to throw in the towel."

"You're holding back. Keep trying."

"I'm. Not. Holding. Back."

"You don't think you are holding back, but you've been burying this ability for years. So, you're holding back. You just don't know it."

"You don't know, either."

"That's true, but we still have to do it."

"UUUrrgghhh. I'm done." I sat up and started undoing the funny boots. I'd walk back to the penthouse barefoot if I had to.

I looked up when Cormac stood. "We'll take a break for today and try again tomorrow night."

"No can do. I've got a shift tomorrow night."

He flipped the switch off, and my still tied boots were suddenly free. "I'll get Arnold to cover your shift. This is more important."

"I understand that money might not be a

concern to you, but it is to me. I'm working tomorrow."

"I'll pay you whatever you make a shift." He stood in front of me.

"No. I'd rather work. This sucks. I'm not good at it and neither of us have any idea if we can even make it work." I went to step around him, since he wouldn't move.

"I'll pay you twice what you make on a busy night," he countered, as he moved in step with me, continuing to block my way as effectively as a large brick wall.

I thought about it for a minute. That was a hard offer to turn down. Even though school was a cakewalk with the strings Cormac had pulled, I still had to pay for it, and then there was still the rent on the trailer. When I finally got away from these people, I'd need a home.

But, as tempting as the money was, a large part of me was relieved that it hadn't worked today and didn't want to keep at it. I didn't want to be involved in this, and I didn't want to help other creatures into the world, that could, possibly, one day turn on humans and destroy us. Even if Cormac said a worse alternative could happen if he didn't, I wasn't sure I should believe him. I only had his word for it. I had to keep remembering that.

"No. I can't do it. We've sat here for hours waiting for nothing. I'm going to work tomorrow night."

"Fine, I'll give you tomorrow night off, but the night after we need to try again."

It bought me time, so I agreed. Maybe I'd make an exit before then. I decided that this wasn't worth the information I was maybe going to get. It didn't look like I was going to be any help to the situation so why hang around and get killed?

Chapter Thirteen

"Help! Cormac!" I'd woken up with something hard pressed firmly against me. It had felt like a wooden board until I opened my eyes and realized I was pressed up against the ceiling. That's when I had started screaming.

"Jo?" Cormac said as he ran to my room. "Open the door!"

I locked it every night. "I can't, I'm..." before I could finish, the door lay splintered half on the frame and half on the floor. Cormac stood there, in loose sleep pants and nothing else, looking like a warrior, with a physique to match, ready to do battle.

He looked up and immediately relaxed. "You scared the shit out of me" he said. "Why the hell did you scream like that?"

"Really? You need me to explain?"

"For someone who wears the most banged up sneakers I've ever seen, you sure like expensive lingerie."

I was so distressed about being stuck to the ceiling, I didn't care I was wearing a silk black teddy that was cut very high and very low.

"You have to help me. I can't get down." I was trying not to sound whiney, but I was pretty sure I failed.

"You just need to relax. Once you do, you'll drop back down," his voice had an odd tone as he said this.

"Don't you dare laugh at me," I said trying to sound fierce but I missed by a mile.

I closed my eyes, did yoga breathing and imagined myself on a sunny beach. All while I remained glued to the ceiling. I opened my eyes and looked pathetically to Cormac.

I watched him, as he stepped onto the bed. "I know you get agitated when people touch you."

"No, I don't." His touch did agitate me, just for a different reason than he thought.

"Yes, you do. I'm going to leech off some of the energy you're producing."

"Just do it."

He reached up and ran his hand along the length of my leg, and I felt a strange sensation, like the bubbles of champagne popping against my skin. Then before I had any warning, I wasn't stuck to the ceiling anymore.

Cormac caught me on my way down, not that he needed to with the bed beneath us. He let my legs swing down, and my body was flush to his. Sensations bombarded me. The heady feeling of being pressed to him immediately replaced the relief over not being stuck to the ceiling. I looked at him and he was staring at my lips.

"You can let me go, now," I said. I needed to

stop this before it began. If he kissed me, it was game over.

He dropped his arms that had been encircling my back, and I slowly moved away from him. Probably a little too slowly, but hey, nobody's perfect. The way I was feeling right now, I was happy I had been able to pull away at all.

Once I got a comfortable distance away from him, I looked back to see him smirk. The bastard knew he was hot.

"Don't be so happy with yourself. I'm young and single and it's been a while is all," I tried saying it as if it was no big deal.

"Really? How long is that exactly?"

"None of your business." There was no way he knew I'd never had sex. He was definitely bluffing.

"I don't think you've ever had sex. I think you're scared."

"Do you really think you can goad me into sleeping with you?"

"No? Not working?"

"No."

"And here comes the attitude. You were much cuter when you were stuck to the ceiling saying 'help me, Cormac'."

"Maybe I am a bit rough around the edges, but whose fault is that? Your people abandoned me. I would think you wouldn't be so condescending, considering that."

"Jo, you need to lighten up a little. Not everything is an attack. I understand what it must have been like. I wasn't passing judgment."

"Really? It sure sounded like you were."

"You don't have to fight me at every turn. I could help you." The sincerity in his voice made my senses reel. He meant what he said. But he was still the guy who ordered me shot. Every day I was here, the memory of it seemed to fade a little bit more. But I couldn't forget that I'd be road kill, complete with tire tracks across my back, if I got in the way of what he thought his responsibilities were. He might mean well now, but that could change in a heartbeat. He couldn't be trusted.

"Think about it. In the mean time, we are training tomorrow at eight. I'm canceling your shift."

"Did you get me any answers yet?" I asked, as I tried to find any reason I could to cancel.

"Not yet, but I should have something by tomorrow night. I'll tell you then." He smiled, knowing he had me, and walked out of my room.

Chapter Fourteen

Ever since I'd gotten stuck to the ceiling last night, I'd been terrified to go outside. The only thing I could imagine was floating away into the clouds. No one had been guarding the door to the penthouse all day, it was the perfect opportunity to get of there, and now, instead of making a dash for it, I was afraid of turning into a helium balloon and popping. This was beyond Murphy's Law. Lately, I felt like Murphy had written my entire life's script.

I was staring out the windows in the living room when Dodd strolled in.

"Hey, Jo! What are you up to?"

I kept looking at the pretty clouds, wondering how far up I'd get before I'd drop. "Why do you keep talking to me like we are friends?"

"You can seriously hold a grudge."

"Only when I'm crossed."

"Okay, let's just settle this already. Here!"

I turned, just as he threw a gun at me. I screamed but caught it anyway. "Is this loaded?"

"What's the point of carrying otherwise?"

I looked at him, wearing a large sweatshirt and jeans. He looked like a kid.

"Hey, psycho, maybe you shouldn't throw it?"

"If five right to the noggin didn't take you out,

do you really think a stray would do it?"

He made a good point.

"Now, shoot me."

"It's not the same. You know you won't die."

"Yes, that's true. But it doesn't make it pleasant."

I pondered the idea for a minute, and found I liked it. "Fine, but this doesn't make us even."

I looked him over, deciding on where I was going to take my shot.

"Hang on, let me go stand near the bar where it's tiled. I don't know how many more couches Cormac has in storage." He crossed the room and stood there, arms out, and motioned that he was ready.

I aimed and shot him in the kneecap, and he immediately collapsed on the ground groaning.

"Really? The knee? That was just mean!"

"What's going on?" Buzz walked into the room and looked at Dodd on the floor and then to me.

"I let her shoot me to even up," Dodd said still groaning from the floor.

Before I even thought about it, I shot Buzz in the knee, and then the other one, before he'd even had time to collapse.

"Awww! Why did I get two?" Buzz said, now lying next to Dodd.

"Because you pulled the trigger."

"Gotta give it to her, she's got a lot of natural

talent," Dodd said, as he lay near Buzz.

As I watched them both squirming on the floor, I realized I did actually feel better. It probably wasn't the therapy a professional would recommend, but it worked better than I could have imagined.

Three hours later Buzz, Dodd, Ben and I were playing Texas Hold'Em and doing shots of tequila. I still didn't trust them. I wasn't even sure if I liked them, but I decided I didn't hate them.

We'd had a long heart to heart after they had eventually been able to get off the floor. In their minds, they had done what was needed to keep everyone safe. It was part of the contract negotiated between the Keepers and the other races they transported. Any human witnesses were to be killed. It was negotiated long before any of them had been born. If humans found out about the portal, and the other races, they'd bring in the army.

Tracker, the man I'd seen turn into a werewolf, didn't get his name by accident, I was told. He was among the most viscous of his group and one that didn't let anything slide by.

"What happened to everybody's pants?" Cormac asked. We all turned from our poker and shots to where he stood in the doorway.

"Retribution, it's not a pretty thing" Dodd explained.

143

Cormac nodded, not asking anything else about it. "Jo, if I could pry you away for a moment, I need a word."

I put my poker hand face down upon the felt of the table Dodd had ordered set up by the windows. "Don't look at my cards. I'll know."

I followed Cormac into his area of the apartment, the half I'd never seen. The living room and bar area were what I considered neutral territory. My room was my sanctuary.

I'd discovered there was no kitchen the first time I was hungry, but considering that I could order anything I wanted, at any time of night and have it within minutes, I quickly understood the lack of one. Cormac seemed far from domesticated. The urge to cook had probably never struck him.

As we walked down the hallway to his area, there was a large bedroom to my left with its door wide open. From my quick glance, it was done in dark browns and navy. An enormous bed played center stage. I breathed a sigh of relief, as we walked past that room. He opened the next door on the left, to what was an office. Bookcases lined the walls, and a large, impressive, wooden desk sat in front of another wall of windows.

He pulled out a chair for me before he sat down behind the desk.

"Well?" I asked.

144

"We hit a couple of snags checking into things. You're definitely half Keeper, but we can't seem to trace who your parent is. We believe it's because the genetics from the other side of your lineage has corrupted the line too much to be distinguished.

"There are several races that come in through the portal. Most of them you've heard of in some variation or form, because as much as there are rules in place for secrecy, over the centuries things have leaked out. I told you Vitor is of a race that human's would refer to as Fae, and that is what the other part of your lineage is. It wasn't obvious at first because our blood is dominant, and for the most part, wipes out all other traits. Problem is it mingles just enough to obscure any answers. To be honest, I'm not sure how I missed it initially. You've got Fae eyes. I knew they were different, it just didn't click at first."

I leaned back in my chair contemplating what that meant for me. I felt like every day, no matter what I did or didn't do somehow I was dragged deeper into this mess. "So, in other words you can't give me any answers?" I asked, aggravated by the situation. Finding out I had some alien Fae blood running through me didn't even daunt me at this point, after what I'd seen lately, nothing was really a shock. What bothered me was, if I didn't know who my mother was, how would I ever find

145

out who had attacked her? And I realized at that moment, my motives had changed. I had always wanted to know what I was, now I wanted to know who had hurt her. She hadn't wanted to leave me. If she had, she would have done it as soon as I was born. She had been hurt and on the run. She'd been trying to protect me from whoever was hurting her.

The only thing I knew now was that she was Fae. If she had been one of the Keepers, she would have healed pretty quickly, maybe even before she made it to the church. The priest had also said I had her eyes, Fae eyes. So my father was the Keeper. And as of right now, he was suspect number one on my list of who hurt her.

"It just means it's going to be a slower process. Is that a problem?" Cormac's voice jarred me back to the present.

I knew what problem he was referring to, was I still willing to help him. "My ability to contribute seems to be going slower than predicted as well, so I guess it's a wash." I didn't add that my options for getting information were limited, at the moment. He knew that, anyway. I didn't feel the need to tell him that I was now afraid to leave the building.

"I see you're making friends?" The chair scraped against the hardwood floor as he stood, his muscular frame silhouetted by the late afternoon sun behind him. Even in the shadows, I detected a smug smile on his face.

"Hardly," I scoffed.

"I'm glad. It's good," he said, disregarding my answer.

"Don't speak to me like that."

"Like what?" He seemed honestly bewildered by my tone.

"Like you know what's best for me."

"I'm sorry, you're right. Don't talk to anyone and don't make friends. It's horrible," he mocked.

"You are a condescending ass."

"And I can see your claws are back out, so why don't we just cut this conversation short and get to work. I don't want you all prickly when you need to focus."

I watched as he walked to the door and held it open for me.

"You have no idea what you're even doing, do you?"

"You're right. I've got no idea what your problem is, now."

"You try to manage me. I've gotten along perfectly well for…"

"Yes, yes, I know. You need no one. You're an island unto yourself."

I walked over to the door and paused next to him before I walked out. "Go ahead, mock me, but don't kid yourself. I've lived alone my whole life and playing nice for a couple of hours with your

147

buddies doesn't change anything. I don't need them. And more importantly, I don't need you!"

I saw something in his eyes harden and a muscle in his jaw twitch. I'd pissed him off. Good. I was sick of him treating me like a pawn that he could maneuver whatever way he chose. It might not have been the brightest move on my part, but god, it felt good. I had a history off chopping my nose off to spite my face. It was nice to know I was still the same girl.

When we got back to the living room, Cormac was visibly annoyed. When he asked who was coming with us to train, both Dodd and Buzz backed out.

"What the hell did you do now?" Dodd asked the second Cormac was out of earshot, having left to go change.

"It's not my fault he's all pissy, and why are you walking so funny?" I couldn't help but notice his odd gait across the room.

"It's totally you, and you're the reason I'm walking funny, too. I think my kneecap fused back funny. Now, I'm going to have to go get them re-broken by the doc."

"You can't get mad now. You said I could shoot anywhere." Before I could defend myself any further, Cormac was back.

He didn't speak, just walked toward the door. I didn't care. I didn't want to talk to him anyway.

Cormac and I spent the rest of the night not speaking, while we stared at rubber balls that wouldn't move.

Chapter Fifteen

"What do you think of this?" I asked Buzz, holding up a charcoal grey cashmere sweater dress. "Do you think it would be flattering? I hate trying stuff on."

"It's great. Can we go soon?"

"Why, is this boring you?"

"No, I love it." I'd never known Buzz was capable of such sarcasm. It made me laugh.

This was the fifth shopping trip this week. Every since I'd had words with Cormac, there had been more tension than ever. Now we seemed to be wrapped up in a tit for tat battle. He'd canceled all my shifts, saying that training was more important. I'd retaliated to his power grab by dragging his men shopping and spending thousands on clothes daily.

Only problem was, the expenditures didn't seem to bother him. I'd changed tactics two days ago. I'd always been told I was beautiful and I wasn't beyond using what I had. I knew that he found me attractive, so I'd stopped wearing jeans and sneakers every day. Skirts and dresses, stilettos and perfume were my new arsenal. I could see him watching me, and I acted like I barely knew he was in the room.

He was a man with a large ego. I couldn't

really blame him for it. He had classic chiseled features, coloring to die for, and a body that would win competitions. It was just plain gluttony that he was rich and powerful too. He was used to women falling at his feet, and I knew that it drove him a little crazier every time he saw me that I seemed to be over any attraction I had felt. Not that I was, but boy, was I getting good at faking it.

"Oh, no! You're not getting that one!"

I looked over at Buzz, then back at the silky red dress in my hands. "You're right, this one is perfect. Do you think the red shoes I got on Monday would match?"

He didn't answer, just groaned. All the guys seemed to be aware of what I was doing, even though I held to my denials. Every guy but Cormac, that was. It was strange, considering he seemed like he was a bright man in every other matter.

"I can't take this anymore. I'll be on the bench."

"Yes, you should relax. I need some new lingerie after this, and I don't want to tire you out." I watched Buzz shake his head, as he went to sit outside the store. Cormac always had someone tailing me everywhere I went. Sometimes I liked to mess with them and make them go shopping with me. None of them ever said no. Cormac must have told them they had to be nice to me.

Try as I might, I couldn't seem to stay mad at

Buzz. He was sort of a likeable oaf once you got to know him. Buzz sat himself on the bench outside, opened the newspaper that he always seemed to have handy, and settled himself in.

He was so engrossed in what he was reading he was oblivious to Vitor when he sauntered into the store. I knew it wasn't a coincidence. I could read it on his face as he strolled over to me. He didn't rush at me, but his attention was focused like a laser, unwavering from my direction.

"You are looking quite beautiful," Vitor said in his cultured voice, as he looked me up and down.

It was an appreciative look from a handsome man. This is what I imagined normal felt like. Too bad he was an alien, and I, the half breed who was the key to opening up other dimensions.

The page I'd gotten from the priest suddenly popped into my head, Golden child born and left, will be the hope of the bereft. Was Vitor the bereft? What if the page actually meant something? Was I supposed to be helping him? I turned toward him now with even more questions burning in my head, but simply said, "Thank you," not sure exactly how to broach the subject.

"So, how have you been?"

"Good." Besides the recent case of agoraphobia, not being completely human, having just recovered from five bullets in the head, and possibly being the subject matter of a very dire sounding prophecy, it was roughly accurate. It was odd, considering the circumstances, to be talking to him as if we just happened to be casual acquaintances. "And how are you?" I didn't add, *are you feeling especially bereft today?* Even though I wanted to.

"I'm doing well. I've heard that you are residing with Cormac?"

I nodded.

"I'm sorry if I scared you last time I saw you. It wasn't my intention."

"I know," I said and meant it.

"I want you to understand, I'm not trying to hurt Cormac. I just believe that it isn't right for him to hold all the cards."

"I think you misunderstand my relationship with Cormac." I hung the red dress back up on the rack.

"I need you to know, I don't want this for myself. I just want to help my people."

I felt the fabric of another dress, as I pondered his words. He was sounding pretty bereft. "I really don't know what I can do." I might be the key for him, but I had no idea how to open the lock.

"I don't know how much he's explained to you, but for reasons you may or may not know about, he's unmovable. There is no talking to him. I need someone that can operate a portal."

"My skills in that area seem to be stunted." I

153

walked to the next aisle, and glanced over at Buzz.

"He's not paying any attention," said Vitor. "Are you afraid of me? Do you want me to leave?"

I turned back and could see the sadness in his eyes. "No, you don't scare me. I don't know why." I shrugged my shoulders. "Maybe you should, but you don't. That doesn't mean that some of the things you tell me aren't always so comfortable."

He smiled slightly and the tension relaxed in his shoulders. "Good. I wouldn't want you to be. I'm not a bad guy, Jo." He lifted his hand and pushed a wayward blond strand behind my ear.

Just as he was pulling his hand back, a movement by the door caught my eye just in time to see Cormac walk in. Walking actually might be too sedate of a word, storming was more like it. His face was set in stone, his eyes as cold as I'd ever seen, the kind of cold that burned.

Cormac didn't stop until he was at my side. He slipped an arm around my waist and pulled me into his side. I instinctively moved to pull back, but his arm didn't budge. I then noticed Vitor's face. I had to give the guy credit, he had guts to be willing to stand up to Cormac.

Cormac wasn't the type of guy other men wanted a problem with, but Vitor would do it. I relaxed into Cormac's embrace and hoped that would ease the quickly growing tension. The moment I did, I regretted it, not because it felt bad,

154

but because it felt too good.

"I thought it wasn't like that?" Vitor asked looking at me.

"Doing a little shopping?" Cormac asked Vitor.

"You could say that." Gone was the gentleman as Vitor eyed me from head to toe.

I knew Cormac didn't want Vitor around me but he was acting like a jealous boyfriend. The tension was so thick I was about to choke on it. Trouble was about to break out any moment. I'd seen violence in my life, but the idea of Vitor beaten into a bloody pulp hit me in a soft spot that I didn't know I had.

"I'm done shopping. Let's go."

I looked from Cormac to Vitor. Neither of them budged.

I spoke again in harsher tones, "You both want something from me, you do this here and now, and neither of you will be getting anything."

Cormac's arm loosened, then fell from my waist as he stepped closer to Vitor. I watched in horror as I tried to decide how much I really did care for Vitor. In reality, I barely knew him. Did I feel for him enough to step in the middle of these two? No, probably not.

I watched Cormac get within an inch of Vitor's face.

"You don't have a shot in hell of taking me on and you know it. You got lucky. Remember that.

You won't get lucky again."

He turned toward me and I quickly walked toward the store exit. I didn't need to check to see if he was following me because I felt his hand rest at the small of my back.

Buzz finally looked up from his paper to realize something was wrong and Cormac waved him off without a word. We walked briskly through the casino. I knew how this would look to all who were watching. We screamed couple with him at my side. The gossip would kick into high gear now, it didn't matter if it was correct or not. Once you could blow off. Twice? Nah, not likely. No one would buy it after being seen a second time like this. There was nothing to be done about it.

Cormac and I stepped into the elevator that would take us to his penthouse, and I watched the doors close. The moment they closed, I felt Cormac's hands grab me. The elevator wall was suddenly at my back and his body pressed full length against me. I opened my mouth to say no, but his mouth was on mine before I got the words out. By the time he moved downward toward my neck, the only noises coming from me were unintelligible, with no resemblance to anything close to no.

I knew we should stop, and I was going tell him to any second. His strong masculine hands ran up my legs toward my hips, and dragged my dress

up with them. I should have told him to stop at
that point, but I didn't and he started kissing me
again. Then his hands circled around and grasped
my ass, pulling my lower body closer to him as
his leg moved in between mine. His thigh pressed
intimately against me and instead of pushing him
away, my hands pulled him closer, as my fingers
intertwined in his dark locks.

One hand climbed upward and cupped my
breast, the other reached around the back of my
thigh lifting it to his side as he ground what felt like
a very large erection against me. I arched my back,
sighed in pleasure and pressed myself into him.

I wasn't aware the elevator doors opened
until he pulled back and grabbed my hand as he
walked forward. I watched his back as we walked
toward the penthouse and panicked. If I didn't stop
it now, I'd never stop it. The door loomed ahead of
me and I pulled my hand out of his. I knew if I
didn't stop this now, I wouldn't once he was
touching me, again.

He stopped instantly, and turned toward me.
"What's wrong?"

"This isn't a good idea," I said, then steeled
myself for his reaction. He stood silent and
unreadable, and I held myself firm, consciously
avoided the urge to fidget.

"Okay."

Was that it? He was going to let it drop that

easily? I watched his back as he opened the penthouse door. He gazed back at me, as I stood frozen for a moment. Was he bluffing? Was he going to maul me the moment I walked in the door? That made no sense. He could do it in the hallway. Even if his men showed up, they wouldn't stop him.

"You're not upset?"

"You're scared. I get that. I'm not some monster who's going to rush you."

Anger gave me the momentum to get my feet moving. "I'm not scared. It's just not a good idea."

"Why are you angry? I'm trying to be understanding about this. You don't need to be defensive."

"I'm not defensive. I won't sleep with you because it's a bad idea." I threw my purse on the couch in a slight huff.

"That, I could understand, but that's not the reason."

"And you know my reasons better than me?"

"I know you want me as much as I want you and I think you are clinging to any reason you can find to... hey, where you going?"

Ignoring him, I slammed the door to my room. He was completely off base.

I sat in the huge Jacuzzi in my bathroom until my skin pruned, but it still didn't relax me. When I finally crawled out, I found a turkey club, a bag of salt and vinegar potato chips, and my favorite flavored latte sitting on the table near my bed. A little note lay on my pillow.

Be ready at eight. Make sure you eat.
Cormac

Nothing worked. It wasn't as if I could operate anything, but he still wanted to keep trying. Nothing stopped that.

I considered ignoring it. The idea of sitting with him alone in a room all night made me distinctly uneasy. Anger prickled at me and I couldn't seem to contain it. Who was he to set the rules? I threw on a robe and left my room, ready to do battle.

"Did you find anything on my parents?" I demanded after I tracked him down in his office. When I felt uneasy, I did what came naturally. I picked a fight.

"No, but I've got men on it."

"That was the deal," I said. I leaned both hands on the desk where he sat.

"And I'm going to get you answers, but I don't remember telling you it would be quick."

I watched as he stood up and circled the desk, and I turned with him as he walked around to my side until he stood in front of me, his desk at the back of my legs. He stood so close his clothes brushed the front of my robe. I couldn't help but breath in his scent. He was wearing a dress shirt, like always, and I found my eyes drawn to the skin at the top of his chest. I could clearly see the definition of his chest. An image of him standing shirtless flashed in my brain, and my breathing hitched.

He stepped closer still. With no room left to back up, I ended up half sitting on his desk. His hands gripped my hips, sliding me farther onto its surface as he stepped in between my legs.

He leaned his head down toward my ear and took my lobe into his mouth, then nipped at the sensitive skin below. "Hmmm, I think I just discovered a way to…"

Ben yelled his name from the other room before he could finish.

His eyes stared into mine for a moment, then he leaned back from me and rested his hip on his desk. I jumped off, fearing I'd look guilty standing anywhere near him.

"I'm in the office," he called out.

Ben's tall lanky frame filled the doorway. "Dodd told me that Tracker is insisting on having his man come over tonight."

"No. I told them no one through this portal until next week. They have to use the other portal."

"Tracker is insisting. He said he's got the

choice of portals. That his man is coming over at nine p.m. What should I tell Dodd to do?"

Cormac pushed off the desk and silently walked the length of the room for a minute.

"Are you ready?" he asked me as he turned back around.

"That's a joke, right?" His face remained stoic. "You couldn't have missed the fact that I haven't been able to do anything?"

"Don't worry about that. I've got an idea."

"An idea? That's certainly reassuring. What if you do it and kill this guy like the last one?"

"I told you, I can't reveal that I don't have control of the portal. It could make things worse."

"I'm not doing it. I want nothing to do with this."

He crossed the room to stand in front of me. "I can't show weakness. If I do, this will only get worse. I can't risk losing any of my people because they are scared."

"Why can't you just say no?"

"Because there is a contract in place set up a very long time ago and it's not one I can break. If they insist, I have to do it or I'll never be able to keep things under wraps. I need to know who's working against me and get to them before this blows up."

"What is it with you and these contracts? It's a piece of paper!"

161

"If I don't keep it open, there will still be bloodshed, and more than one person might die. I need to bring the guy through and I need it to work."

"I've worked very hard to get my life on a normal track. I don't want to be involved in your mess!"

"You keep saying that like this isn't your heritage, just as much as mine. I don't have a choice and neither do you. Just because you didn't know about it, and I did, doesn't make it any more mine. This is who you are. You need to stop running at some point and own it."

"If I do this, I want the tails off me and I'm moving back home. I'm tired of being followed everywhere I go. I'm done with your rules. You want me to be a team player than you better start treating me like one."

"They aren't there to watch you. They're there to protect you."

"I don't care. I want them gone."

He stood there unmoving, and I didn't know if it was going to go my way or not.

"Fine, but you stay here."

"No."

He leaned in, taking a large chunk of my personal space up. Cormac was good at intimidation tactics like that. "I don't have to negotiate."

"Considering that you need me, I think you do." I knew it, and I'd press for all I could. It was now or never.

He took my chin in a gentle grasp as he tilted my face to his and said in a near whisper, "Don't push it. I can do this without you being willing."

"You can?" I asked in a surprised tone not much louder than his.

He nodded.

"Then why haven't you done it already?"

"That doesn't matter. Just know that I can."

I jerked my face out of his grasp. "Fine, but we lose the guards."

"Fine."

He picked up the phone on the desk and dialed a number into it. "Tell him that we're bringing his guy over." The phone clanked loudly on its holder in the silent room.

Chapter Sixteen

"Where is everyone?" I asked Dodd as we entered the empty portal room several hours later. Last time we had been down here, the place had been hopping.

"If this goes bad, I want as few witnesses as possible," Cormac answered for him. "It's only going to be us three."

"How 'bad' can this go?" It was a little late to ask, but what the hell. I looked at both of them but suddenly they seemed to be too distracted to pay attention. "Oh yes, now I feel good. So, how does this work exactly? Since I never got past getting the balls in the air, I'm not sure what I'm going to be able to do for you guys."

"Oh, don't sell yourself short there darling, you could…" Dodd fell deathly quiet, and I looked over to see the stare Cormac was leveling at him, his veins twitching. "Oh come on! I was only playing."

Cormac looked back down at the computer in front of him. "Dodd and I are going to try to channel some of your ability."

"Does that work?"

"Sometimes. I think it will this time. When you were stuck on the ceiling the other night, I drained you, that's how I got you down."

164

I heard what sounded like a giggle from Dodd, and I leveled my own death stare at him. "I'd shut up before I shoot out your knee caps, again."

"Really? This is how the night is going to go? You guys need to lighten up. Maybe if you two…"

"Dodd!" Cormac didn't give him a chance to finish.

"I canceled a date tonight with Vicky for this," Dodd said.

"I thought Vicky was with you?" I looked over at Cormac.

"She's mad about you staying at the penthouse," Dodd now answered for Cormac, who stood silently.

"Why would you date her if she's involved with Cormac?"

"Cormac gave me the thumbs up. He wasn't interested in her seriously, and now I get some revenge sex." I must not have hidden my thoughts well.

"Hey, no judgment! You don't know how hard it is for a guy to turn down revenge sex."

"Let's get in position," Cormac said, as I still grimaced over Dodd's comments. "Dodd, hold her other hand," Cormac said as he held my right.

"Got it, Boss."

There we stood, lined up in front of where I imagined the portal would open, Cormac on my right and Dodd on my left.

"Jo, just try to stay relaxed. I'd imagine it's going to feel slightly odd."

"You'd imagine? You mean you don't know?"

"No, we're flying blind here."

"Great."

Cormac closed his eyes and I watched around the room, not sure what I was waiting for. Then I saw it, it looked like a flicker of an electrical charge, the kind you saw when you drag your foot across the carpet or touch something in the dark. But, it didn't go away; it stayed centered between the monoliths of ebony, flickering. Then it grew, and grew. As it got larger, a gentle breeze filled the room, and blew my hair from my face.

I turned and looked at Cormac whose eyes were wide open now and focused ahead. Dodd had a similar look upon his face. I watched as this weird entity opened larger and larger, until it took up almost the entire wall, stretching from monolith to monolith. It was actually quite beautiful, and then the oddest thing started to happen, its surface, which had looked sparkly before, started to clear. A shade of lavender shimmered behind the flickering. Then I realized that the portal wasn't lavender, but the sky of the world I was seeing into. There was a thing I would describe as a moon if I saw it hanging here, but it was enormous compared to Earth's. A silhouette of a man appeared against the strange sky. He walked toward us, and I felt the room heat up. The heat poured at us in waves. I felt like it was seeping into my bones, like I'd been roasting on the beach with the sun hanging in noon position for five hours straight.

The man slowly emerged clearer into view. He couldn't have been more than twenty. He looked like a surfer with shaggy blond locks hanging over one eye. He stepped through the portal and greeted us with a brilliant white smile that could have been on a Crest toothpaste ad.

The portal closed quickly once he stepped through, snapping shut into nothing, but I could feel the energy rolling through the room. Then it hit me like a punch in the gut. Sweat was streaming down my face and it was an effort to remain upright.

"Did you feel the close?" Cormac asked Dodd.

"No," he replied a bit ominously, and they both turned and looked at me.

"Get him out of here," Cormac said stiffly, and Dodd escorted surfer dude out while I struggled to stand.

"How do you feel?"

"I'm fine," I replied through gritted teeth.

"No you aren't. I think you got the full blast."

"Huh?" The feeling of running my intestines through a meat grinder made it hard to concentrate.

"I need to get you upstairs."

167

"I'm fine." Even as I said it, I knew what I must have looked like. I could feel the cold sweat on my face. With the way I was feeling, I knew my skin had probably gone from golden tan, to ashen white. The feeling of vulnerability was suffocating me.

"I know you don't trust me, but I'm telling you now, you can."

He put an arm around my waist and tried to help support my weight. I used the last of my strength to pull away. I managed to walk a couple of steps to lean against the nearby wall, feeling too sick to stay upright without some help. I watched him take off his dress shirt and then the white undershirt, and then he shrugged back into his dress shirt. He grabbed his discarded white undershirt and approached me.

"I'm sorry, but I don't have anything else. It's clean. I just put it on right before we came down here," he said before he used it to wipe the sweat from my face. "Let me help you. I promise, no matter what, I won't let anything happen to you." He looked into my eyes then, "You don't have to believe me. Time will tell."

"No, it won't. I'm not going to be here long enough."

He didn't respond, just patted my face with the soft white cotton. It smelled of him, and I liked it. I pushed his hand away.

"You ready? I need to get you out of here now, the longer we wait the worse it will be."

"Why?" I asked, the pain seemed to subside slightly, and before he could answer, another round struck me that doubled me over and made me gasp for air.

"That's why."

He leaned down and slung my arm around his shoulder, taking practically all my weight. This time I didn't have it in me to fight. The hallway outside the room was empty, so was the elevator that would take us up several floors, but I'd have to make it out of that one and through the casino hall and into the penthouse elevator, all while appearing normal though my insides now felt like someone had shot napalm into them.

"The doors are going to open in ten seconds. Are you ready? Can you do this?"

I nodded, took a deep breath, and stood up straight.

The walk took forever, or in real time, about three minutes. I just concentrated on not crumbling to the ground, one foot in front of the other. Cormac had his hand on my back, slightly steering me and it was a godsend. Even though my eyes were open, my entire attention was on not passing out from the pain.

We stepped into the elevator, and I felt Cormac's arm go around my waist again and I slumped against him.

"You did good," he said, and I thought he kissed my head but I wasn't sure, in my current state.

"What's wrong with me?" I asked into his shoulder.

"You got too much radiation."

"I thought radiation was no big deal?"

"Too much of anything can be bad. All three of us were pulling at it, but you absorbed it all. You've got an unusually strong pull. I'm so sorry, I had no idea that could happen."

"Is this going to kill me?"

"No."

"You don't know do you?"

"I won't let it."

"How long will this pain last?"

"A day or so, I think. You're a lot smaller than the guys it has happened to. I don't know if body weight plays into it."

When the elevator doors slid open, he reached down to pull me into his arms.

"No, I can walk."

He didn't argue with me, just scooped me up into his arms anyway. I didn't pay attention as we walked into the penthouse, just leaned against him with my eyes closed, as I tried to ride out another wave of pain.

I felt the bed against my legs as he laid me

down and then curled onto my side. I felt Cormac's hands as he pulled off my shoes, and I pulled my knees inward and tucked them up against my body. Curled into a ball in the center of the bed, I opened my eyes when I heard him talking in hushed tones. That's when I realized I wasn't in my room, but his.

I tried to sit up, I needed to get to my own room, but hands pressed me back into the mattress before I made any real progress.

"Jo, I've got someone coming to check on you. Just lie back and relax."

I didn't want to lie back, but the pain gripped me with an iron fist so tightly that I didn't have a choice.

An undistinguishable amount of time later, I heard a soft female voice whisper near me. I opened my eyes to see a beautiful brunette with a kind smile hover over me before I shut them again. I felt her soft touch upon my head as she felt for the pulse in my wrist. The hallmark cold metal on my chest told me she was listening to my lungs.

"She'll be fine. It's just going to be an unpleasant night for her," the feminine voice said.

"Isn't there something you can give her?" Cormac's voice asked.

"No. It's not safe with the overload of radiation. Try heating pads or a warm bath. That might help with the muscle spasms."

"Thanks for coming so quickly, Sabrina."

171

"No problem. Call me if anything changes."

Opening my eyes again in the dim room, I saw Cormac shut the door. It was just the two of us, now.

"How do you feel?"

"Like I'm on my deathbed?"

"You're not dying."

"I know, but right now, I almost wish I was."

I closed my eyes and tried to ride out the pain with as much dignity as I could muster. I felt the mattress near me sink down, strong arms wrapped around me, pulling me into Cormac's side.

"Just try to relax," he said.

Even with the pain, my brain was still aware of his hard muscular body lying next to me. His hand was slowly rubbing my back and the pain lessoned its hold slightly.

"Are you doing something?"

"I'm trying to. I can't take it all from you, but I might be able to take the edge off."

The last thing I remembered was my cheek resting against an impossibly hard chest. I'm not sure how long I passed out, but I woke as excruciating pain radiated through the length of me.

I felt Cormac's heat pressed against me, and I realized he must have stayed with me the whole time, however long that was. My body tensed with the next wave of pain, and I felt Cormac move out

172

from under me. My fingers gripped his shirt without meaning to.

"I'll be right back."

For the first time in a long while, I was truly scared to be alone, and I really started to wonder if I was, indeed, dying. I heard the water running in the adjoining bathroom, and I couldn't help but resent that I while I lay in pain caused by helping him, he was showering.

My resentment was short lived, as he walked back in the room shirtless, with just a pair of gym shorts on. He looked like a dark angel come to collect me.

"What are you doing?" I asked, as he picked me up in his arms.

"Heat, the doctor said the heat would help."

The bright lights of the bathroom hit my eyes before he dimmed them quickly. I heard the humming of what sounded like a hot tub. He lowered us both, and I felt the hot water soak through my clothes as he sat down with me still in his arms. The water felt like it was almost boiling, and it was fantastic, reducing the intensity of the spasms within minutes.

As the cramping started to subside, I became acutely aware that much of Cormac's naked skin pressed against me; the way the material of my shirt clung to my breasts detailed every curve. I turned to look into Cormac's face, just mere inches away, and I could see I wasn't the only one who was becoming very aware.

I grabbed the edge of the tub, splashing water everywhere with my sudden movement and pulled myself out. I barely stopped long enough to grab a towel in my rush from the room, leaving a watery trail behind me as I ran into my room and collapsed on my bed.

"Jo?" Cormac said as he stood just inside my door. "I don't want to leave you alone."

"I'm fine. The pain is subsiding." I rolled on my side and looked away from him. I didn't want to be alone anymore, but I couldn't trust him. I'd been getting sloppy. I'd relaxed my guard. I couldn't afford to do that. I still had no idea who my parents were, what had happened to my mother that night long ago. Cormac had his own priorities. It didn't matter what he said, he'd had me hurt once, he'd do it again. Actions were what were important.

"No, you aren't." I felt the bed dip as he climbed in next to me. His arm pulled my body close to his, and I didn't fight it, but just lay there nestled alongside him.

Chapter Seventeen

I woke alone the next afternoon to a beautiful Monet painting leaning against the wall, opposite the bed. It was beautiful, with red lily clusters. I wasn't sure why it was sitting there but I wasn't going to complain.

The need for a strong cup of coffee propelled me toward the living room in hopes that Cormac might have a pot of hazelnut floating around.

"So, what are we going to do?" I heard Dodd ask as I neared the room.

"I don't know, but she's not doing it anymore. Not like last time. Not until I know it won't happen again. It could have killed her," Cormac replied.

"But we've got the Festiva. What are we going to tell them when we can't get them over?"

"I'll figure something else out." He spoke in a tone that made it clear he was done discussing it.

As I walked in, I saw Cormac standing by the windows while Dodd and Buzz sat on the couch.

"Hey, how are you feeling? Heard you had a rough night?" Dodd asked.

"I'm fine."

"Why am I not surprised?" Dodd asked.

Cormac didn't say a word, but walked over to me. He looked me over a little too intensely for comfort. Even though it wasn't a sexual perusal, I

175

was glad I'd opted for jeans and an oversized sweatshirt.

"How are you going to run the portal?" I asked him.

"It's not your problem."

"If what you said is true, then isn't it everyone's problem?"

"I'll handle it." He turned back to Dodd and Buzz. "I'm going to go see if I can track down Hammond."

"Is he even alive anymore?" Buzz asked.

"Yes, and I'm going to find him," Cormac replied. He turned back to me. "I don't want you going out today. You need to rest."

I tilted my head toward the foyer and motioned for him to follow me.

"What's wrong?" he asked, once we stopped in the foyer and out of earshot.

"I know this isn't the best time to talk, but I have to get this off my chest. I think I've been throwing you some mixed signals, but I just want to make it clear, we are just business. I'll help you through this mess and you'll get me the answers I need, then we go our own way. I'm not looking for any other kind of relationship."

"Sure."

"That's not a problem for you?" I guess he hadn't been that interested then.

"Believe it or not, I've got other options."

"I mean, obviously you do. I just think that this is the way it should be."

"Like I said, no problem."

Completely nonchalant, like it didn't mean a damn thing that I was rejecting him. He did know I was rejecting him, right?

"So, strictly business."

"Yes, and I've got some of that to attend to. Was this all you needed?"

"Yep, that was it."

"Great, see you later!" he said as he walked toward the door, but then paused. "I almost forgot, did you like the painting?"

"It's beautiful. Were you going to hang it on the wall there?"

"Is that where you want it?"

"It's your painting. Hang it wherever you want it."

He smiled. "It's for you."

"I couldn't! It's a Monet! Isn't it?"

"Yes, it is. No strings. I knew you had a rough night so I thought you would like it. It's called *Red Lilies*. I've got to go. See you later."

I stood, still staring at the door as words from the page sprang to mind. Eternal Lilies bloom after a hard night, the giver of gifts will stand for the right. Nope, it was just a coincidence. I wasn't going to start reading into things thinking there were cryptic meanings. There was some strange stuff going on, but I refused to buy into fortune telling, too. A girl had to draw the line somewhere.

I walked back into the living room where Dodd and Buzz still sat.

"Who's Hammond?" I asked, as I refused to let my mind get swept up into crazy thoughts.

"He's an old timer. Crazy strong. He trained Cormac. He was his mentor." Dodd answered.

"And you really think he'll have some answers on how to fix what's happening?"

"He's our best bet."

"Why aren't there anymore older alchemists? Someone with answers? I mean really, you can't die? What happened to them all?"

"We can die. It's just hard to kill us."

"You put five bullets in my head, and I didn't die."

"Okay, so it's really hard, but it can be done. We had something akin to a civil war about twenty years ago."

"And that's when Cormac took control? He must have been barely a kid." It wasn't a question. He was a leader born. Some people lead, but in him it was instinctual. "What were you fighting about?"

"Some of us wanted to use the portal for power over the other races. They felt that we should rule everyone who came over. And then some of the people who did manage to circumvent the system, well, that got ugly."

"Ugly? What was uglier than a civil war?"

"The Fae cursed some of them. They died slowly and painfully. Nobody could do anything because they voided the contract first. That's why nobody messes with the contracts."

"When do all these people for Festiva have to come over by?"

"The next couple of days or it's gonna start getting awkward."

"I still don't understand what exactly is going wrong? Do you guys know?"

"When a portal is opened, it produces a large mass of radiation. One of the things we do is pull that radiation towards us. For some reason, it's not pulling forward like normal and we don't know why. It's lingering within the portal and frying anyone who goes into it."

"What about if someone were to go into the portal while another person operates it. Instead of just pulling from the outside? Would that give you more control?"

"It might, but it's hard when you're in the portal. It screws with your abilities. The person would have to be awfully strong, otherwise they'd fry up."

"Do you think I could do it?"

"Oh, no! Don't even think about it."

"Dodd, just answer me. Do you think I could?"

He made a loud aggravated sigh. "You might be able to. I've seen the power you put out. But Cormac said you couldn't do anything else."

"If we don't fix this, from what I'm being told, all hell will break loose. Is that correct?"

Dodd and Buzz looked at each other hesitantly, then both looked back at me and nodded.

"And then it's not going to be just your world but mine, too, that is in danger."

"You've been kicking and screaming this entire time. Now you want to step up and save the day?"

"Do I want to? Absolutely not. But I'm starting to think I have to. I've met Tracker. Him ruling the world holds no appeal to me."

"Who said it's Tracker? Cormac thinks it's probably Vitor.

"I don't. I want to try and run the portal while I'm inside. Will you help me?"

"You're asking us to go against Cormac. He just said he didn't want you going anywhere near it," Dodd replied.

"Yes, I am, but if Cormac doesn't find Hammond or some other solution soon, we need to try it."

"I don't know," Buzz said looking completely panicked at the idea of going against Cormac.

"You both need to man up," I said. "Cormac will go down with the sinking ship. What good are you doing him? You need to think for yourselves and stop being babies. You aren't hurting him, you're possibly saving his ass."

"She's right. It's not disloyal. There'll be more defectors if we don't get this worked out, and you know Cormac will go down dying before he steps aside," Dodd said.

"Okay, but we give him the week?" Buzz asked.

"And it's got to be the last resort," Dodd added.

"Yes. We give him the week."

Chapter Eighteen

It had been five days and no sign of Hammond. Cormac had only been at the penthouse to sleep. I wondered if he was trying to avoid me, but he hadn't been at the casino either. Dodd and Buzz, my new coconspirators had told me he'd been on the hunt for Hammond every minute of every day.

When I did see Cormac in passing, either late at night or the crack of dawn, I could see the stress was wearing on him. He looked exhausted. Like the weight of the world rested upon his shoulders. From what I had heard, it might be the truth.

Concerned that we would have to enact my plan, I'd woken that day with a new determination. It had taken me about three hours, but I finally found Dodd downstairs near the slot machines. He was in the middle of trying to work a cocktail waitress I didn't recognize, and I wondered if she had been hired to fill my spot.

"We've got to talk," I said to him as I approached the couple.

"Sure, give me a couple of minutes." He turned so that only I could see his face and used his eyebrows to signal he was in the middle of working the new girl.

Rolling my eyes right back, not caring if the girl

saw, I went and stood at the end of the aisle as I watched him try to close the deal with the pretty brunette. She handed him a slip of paper, that I could only assume had her phone number and walked away while they both smiled.

"I've been trying to crack that one for a week," he said, when he came to me. He held up the paper she had handed him, waving it at me. "Sooner or later, they all succumb."

"We've got bigger issues than your sex life."

"Nothing's bigger than my sex life. Sex is very important to me. I won't have you belittling it."

"Dodd, can you stop? We need to plan."

He made a point of sighing loudly and dramatically. "Okay, let's plan."

"Not here."

"Obviously. Let's go to my place. I don't want anyone walking in on this. Cormac will rip me a new one if he hears."

"Lead the way."

We took the penthouse elevators up to the floor beneath Cormac's. His entire place was dark browns, and the biggest TV I'd ever seen dominated one wall.

"We need to do this."

"You know it's very dangerous, right?" he asked, all the earlier playfulness gone.

"Yes, but what's the alternative?"

"And you know you could die doing it? From

what I've heard, you already came close last time."

I'd known it was possible, but it still chilled me to hear. "I figured as much." I sat on his couch as my knees became weak.

"Why are you so set on this? I thought you considered this our problem. You haven't made any secret about the resentment you have toward Keepers." He handed me a shot of what smelled like tequila and sat across from me in an armchair.

"For whatever reason, I'm the only one who might be able to do it. How do I not, knowing what the alternative might be. I didn't want it to be my problem but I don't feel like I have a choice."

"You could just let the whole thing work out however it does, go off and live your life. Even if Tracker took over, it might never become an issue. If it does, you would still have your life. Things might be different, but at least you would be alive to know how it turned out. Your way, you might not see next month."

I just shrugged my shoulders.

"The way I see it, you either have a soft spot for Cormac," he paused to chug back his shot, "or you've got some sort of death wish. I'm not sure which."

I opened my mouth to speak but he held up his hand and interrupted me before I could. "Don't bother arguing. I'm beyond stubborn in my opinions. I can see the way you look at Cormac, so there is no sense denying that. I can also see you're a very unhappy person. We've all got skeletons, but I'm afraid you might have a whole god damn cemetery. I'm going to go through with your plan, mostly because I don't know if we have a choice. What really bothers me though, is that my gut feeling tells me that as much as I sense the fight in you, I'm not so sure you'd run away from death. Making plans with someone like you is dangerous."

I sat there and pondered his words for a moment. If I was the type to self evaluate, I might agree with him. Lucky for me, I wasn't that type. I knew I was an emotional wreck. Problem was I didn't see the point in dwelling on the past. It had already messed me up. Why keep going back for more?

I swigged back my own shot, which I could now confirm was tequila, and asked, "So, does that mean you're in?"

He shook his head no, but his lips said yes.

"I know you do all the scheduling. Whoever you have to bring over, set it up for Sunday. All of them."

"Why Sunday?"

"He's got a lead that is taking him out to LA. He'll be gone all day."

"He doesn't have a lead in LA."

"He will."

He laughed now, but not a cheerful kind. The

kind that was full of nervousness. "Now I know you've got a death wish. Are you insane? You planted a phony lead?"

"It's the only way."

"How do you know he's going to go out there Sunday? What if he follows up on it before then?"

"Won't happen. The lead is only going to be available to talk on Sunday."

"Who is it?"

"Do you really want more details?"

"You know what? You're right. I don't want to know. He's going to kill you."

"He already tried once. It didn't work then."

Dodd went and grabbed the tequila and took a swig right from the bottle, then offered it to me. I accepted.

"Don't tell Buzz, I don't think he'll be able to keep the secret."

"I wish no one had told me." He took the tequila bottle back and took another swig.

Chapter Nineteen

"I've got some news."

I looked over to watch Cormac as he strolled into my room Sunday morning. In a matter of hours, my plan would take effect. I knew I had started to act a bit jittery. I always prided myself on keeping my cool, but that was before I'd landed in this mess. And as far as what I was doing today, I'd never done anything like this before. Cormac wouldn't appreciate being led on a goose chase. If he ever discovered this was a set up, he would lose it.

It didn't matter. I was going to do what I had to, regardless of the outcome and ramifications. If I died, it wouldn't matter how mad he was. If we managed to pull it off, I bought him more time to find out what was going wrong and who was behind it, he'd need me to keep doing. I'd have leverage, not to mention I'd have saved his ass. I mean really, how mad could he be? Now I just had to make sure I had the chance to pull it off.

"What's up?" I tried to sound casual, not moving from my spot leaning against the headboard while I drank my hot coffee.

"The lab managed to determine some of your lineage."

My heart skipped a beat even as I tried to stay

calm. That wasn't what I'd expected at all. "I thought they couldn't do anything with the blood?"

"One of my guys had the smart idea of taking a Fae sample and applying it to all of our genetic lines, seeing if they could rule any out. It worked better than they had even imagined. All Alchemists descend from the original ten. They managed to determine that you are a descendant of Drake."

"Are you a Drake?" The idea of being his cousin made me slightly sick. No one wants to think they'd lusted after a relative. That's just disturbing.

"No."

I took a mental sigh of relief. "So who was Drake?"

"We don't have much information on Drake, or any of the founding ten. A lot of our history was destroyed through the years. Paranoia ran rampant through the alchemists. They were always afraid of revealing secrets. That's how the pact came to be. They bartered with the Fae who had the ability to fuse the knowledge of the alchemists to their actual genes."

"How does that work?"

"It's built into our DNA now, like, the way a bird knows how to fly north. It's a knowledge that is passed down genetically. Problem is it has become less dependable through the years, causing a lot of variations in how strong each descendant is. From the stories that I do know, my belief is that they thought it would be more reliable and consistent than it turned out to be. Perhaps they were led to believe that. I really don't know."

He sat down on the edge of my bed as he talked and really started looking around the room, eyeing several piles of clothes. "Why is your room so messy?"

"Why's yours so neat?"

"Neat is good."

"Personally, I think it's just uptight."

"When was the last time you let the maid in?"

"Yesterday."

"Yesterday? You did this in one day?"

"I tell her not to touch my piles. I can never find anything after she moves my stuff around."

"So this is how you want it?"

"Yes, Cormac, I'm a slob. Is that what you want to hear? Now get off my bed. I want to drink my coffee and watch the news." And don't you have an appointment?

He just shook his head as he stood obligingly. "I'll be back tonight. I've got a lead to check out."

I wanted to jump out of the bed and start getting ready, but I schooled myself until I watched his tall muscular frame walk out the door in search of my fictitious lead. As I heard the main door shut,

I sent Dodd a text message. He was waiting in the hallway less than fifteen minutes later.

"You ready?" he asked.

"I should be asking you that. You're the one with cold feet."

"What happened to your cute outfits?" he asked as we entered the elevator.

"This isn't cute enough?" I smoothed my moist palms down over my skinny jeans, realizing how nervous I really was.

He shrugged. "I like looking at your legs in skirts."

"Sorry to disappoint. I was worried there might be a draft in the portal."

"I was hoping there was." He had the perfect rogue smile on his handsome face. If it had been Cormac, I might have melted on the spot, because he affected me like no one else. However, as handsome as Dodd was, him I could resist.

"Not even a blush? Nothing?"

"I don't blush."

We went the rest of the way going over the times and numbers, until we made it down to the lower hallway. "Where is everyone?"

"How many times do you have to be told that witnesses aren't good? It's bad enough we are going behind his back. I didn't want to take anyone down with us. And if we blow it, I don't want to have to take them out."

"I thought you didn't kill your own?"

"Nah, we don't. I just wanted to sound like a hard ass."

"Dodd, anybody ever tell you that you're a little off?"

"Well, ain't that the kettle calling the pot black."

"So, is this going to really screw up your relationship with Cormac?"

"He's like my brother. I'd do anything for him. I can't sit back and let him shoulder this all on his own." He unlocked the final door and the pillars stood before me, huge, dark, and daunting.

"Okay, little girl, time to see what you've got," Dodd said as he stood next to me.

"Don't worry, I'll bring it. This little girl is about to save your ass." I heard the words I spoke and I sounded tough enough. Just hoped I really did have it to bring. I sure as hell didn't want to step into that portal whistling Dixie.

"I sent a message through for them. They'll be ready in thirty minutes from now."

I pushed up the sleeves of my shirt. "Now, let's just hope I'll be ready." I hadn't meant to say it out loud. Hadn't even realized I had until I saw Dodd's face. "Only kidding, I'm good!" I infused my words with as much bravado as I possibly could, but Dodd's face didn't look any more reassured.

"I'll get it up and running, but I'm not going to

pull at the radiation. That's what went wrong last time. I'll just hold it open. You step in. You're a natural at pulling."

I nodded my head, not wanting to think about what would happen if I didn't just naturally pull the radiation toward me. I thought of all sorts of crispy critters falling out of the portal. Maybe I'd be the crispiest critter of all. Either way, I just wanted to get it over with and let the chips fall as they may, but I had to wait, minute by slow ticking minute, while Dodd fiddled around the room.

When the time finally came, my stomach was churning like I'd been on rough seas all day. I swallowed hard and held on to the contents of my stomach, barely. It was hard to look like a bad ass when you were puking your stomach contents up from nerves.

"You ready?"

"Completely." I was so full of it that I even amazed myself. He smiled and nodded as he took his place and started his end of things. I might have given Dodd a little too much credit if he believed my bullshit.

I put my hands in my pockets to hide their shaking, as I slowly watched the sparks start in the center until it grew larger and larger. Once it spanned the entire distance between the monoliths, I looked over at Dodd who gave me the go ahead. I slowly approached, knowing I dragged my feet, then took a deep breath and took the final step. The one that would either hold this masquerade together, or end it, at least for me.

As I stepped inside, the air tingled all around me and everything blurred slightly. I wasn't sure if it was my eyes or the haze from the portal. A slow breeze picked up, but it wasn't natural, because instead of coming from one direction, it came from every direction. I didn't remember seeing surfer boy's hair blowing when he had come through, but I did remember feeling a breeze last time and I realized it was the radiation flowing to me. Okay, so one problem down, having no clue what I was doing, I was pulling the radiation. Now, as long as it didn't kill me, this would be cake.

Then I looked toward the opening on the other end of the portal, which was about a short city block away. A crowd that looked to be over a hundred, gathered there. Could this be right? I looked at a blurry Dodd, who motioned them to start filing through, unfazed by the number of people.

They were short, tall, fat and skinny. The only thing they had in common was they were all very normal looking. I wouldn't have given them a second glance if I saw them on the street. Some eyed me warily as they passed, and I could tell it was abnormal to have someone standing in the portal, but nobody remarked. That was until a haggard woman, who was a hundred if she was a day, stopped next to me. Her crazy grey hair shot out in every direction.

"You look familiar," she said.

"I don't think I know you."

"I didn't say I knew you." She looked me overly intently, and then walked away, disappearing into the group.

I could see, even from inside the portal, as the crowd paused and then exited the room. That's when I felt it; a pair of eyes on me, my skin broke out in goose bumps. My eyes darted to the door to find Cormac standing there, hours earlier than I had expected him to make it back. His face was unreadable, but his eyes bored into mine as he ignored the crowd of people that parted around him as he walked forward.

I watched as the last few people stepped out of the portal, and I followed them out. Dodd closed it up shortly after I did, but I barely noticed. I kept Cormac in my peripheral vision to the deficit of everything else.

"Hey, watch where you're going," I heard, as I bumped into someone right in front of me.

"Sorry," I said as I looked at a tall lanky, middle-aged man and backed up. I turned back to see if Cormac had noticed and saw his gaze still followed me. He couldn't do anything, I told myself. I was the key to him keeping this operation

194

together.

I waited and watched as the last few people walked through the door. I stood there waiting while I watched Cormac, hand on the doorknob, eye Dodd and tilt his head toward the hallway.

"It wasn't..." Dodd started to say something that I think was going to be in defense of me, but Cormac shook his head and Dodd's voice died midsentence. He hung his head and exited.

He shut the door behind Dodd almost too softly, and I listened to the click of the lock find its home.

"What were you thinking?" he asked, as he paced the room no longer staring at me.

"I think that's obvious isn't it? I was buying you time."

"This could have gone very badly. I can't believe you got Dodd to go along with this." He ran his hand through his hair.

"It wasn't his fault. I twisted his arm. Don't come down on him for this."

He suddenly stopped pacing and looked at me.

"How I handle Dodd isn't any of your business. This," he motioned to encompass the whole room, "is none of your business."

"You say that now, but that's not exactly the truth. You dragged me into this," I made an equally dramatic sweeping gesture that was mocking as

195

well. "I wanted nothing to do with this."

"When I brought you in, I didn't think for one second you would do something this stupid. You could have killed all of them!" He paced angrily across the room, like a lion caged in a pen, his prey just out of reach.

"But I didn't."

A sudden unexpected turn had him inches from my face. His finger pressed just below my collarbone.

"You. Didn't. Know. That." He punctuated each word with his finger.

"And like I said, it worked out fine." I punctuated my own words by shoving his hand away from me.

He grabbed me by the shoulders, my back pressed against the monolith, his body pressed against me, holding me there.

"You could have killed yourself."

"When did I become indispensable? Last time I checked, whether I lived or died wasn't of any large significance."

He didn't say a word, but he also didn't budge. I wasn't sure if he was going to strangle me or kiss me, and I didn't know which scared me more.

"You're done. You aren't to come anywhere near this room again."

"So big shot, how do you plan on running the portal?"

"All balls, no brains. You don't know when to shut your mouth, but it doesn't matter." He leaned in just a hair closer. "You're through." He pushed off the wall and away from me. I took a deep filling breath, and realized I'd barely breathed while he had been so close.

"I think we should go our separate ways," I said to his back, watching as he walked to the door and held it open, waiting for me.

"No. I told you, I can't take the chance of someone else getting their hands on you."

I walked forward and paused in the doorway, and turned to look up into his chilling blue eyes. "I'm done living by your rules. I'm leaving."

"Just try it."

"We'll see." This time, I gave him my back.

Chapter Twenty

"I demand to see her!"

The screaming voice in the hallway woke me from a deep slumber. It was probably the best sleep I'd had since I'd gotten here and I was quite annoyed that I'd been startled from it. I pulled the spare pillow over my head and tried to dull the racket.

"She's not here," I heard Cormac reply. He was lucky I was still too unmotivated to step into the foyer and prove him wrong.

"She's part Fae. I should have been informed the minute you knew that."

That sounded like Vitor's voice. I'd never heard that tone from him before. The fog of sleep slowly started to pull back as what they were saying settled into my brain.

"She's not here."

"You have until tonight to produce her."

"You're more than welcome to come back tonight."

The door slammed and I knew it had to have been Vitor. Cormac wasn't the type of guy who would slam a door in Vitor's face, he'd slam his face. My body didn't want to get out of bed, but I had too many questions I wanted answered to stay here. As I swung my legs over the edge, and was about to make the final push upward, Cormac knocked at my door, effectively bringing the answers to me. Lucky me. I pulled my legs back under the covers, and told him to come in while I waited to hear what splendid news I was in store for.

"Well?" I asked, not bothering to keep my eyes open.

"He wants access to you. Actually, if we want to be more specific, he's demanding access to you."

"God, I'm a popular girl these days." I chuckled, finding myself funny.

"He's going to want to take you with him."

"What?" That got my attention. I jumped into an upright position in bed. "Tell him he can go screw. That goes for you, too. I'm tired of you macho men telling me whether I'm coming or going." I started to feel around the covers of the bed.

"What are you doing?"

"I'm trying to find my phone."

"Why don't you put it on the night stand?"

"I can't. I keep it on vibrate. You ever hear how loud vibrate is on a hard surface? Ah, here it is. Give me his number. I want to call him."

"Remember when I told you that you were part Fae?"

"Yes, you also told me it didn't make a

199

difference because the Alchemist genes were dominant. That it was a nonissue."

"I didn't say it wasn't an issue. You know how humans aren't technically adults until they are eighteen? In the case of Fae, it's twenty-four. He's got a right to you."

"That's all fine and dandy, but we don't live in the purple land with the freaks. We live here on Earth where he has no rights."

"But we are still bound to certain rules and…"

"If you start bringing up contracts, I'm going to throw this phone at your head." I even went as far as to raise my hand and aim it.

"There is no reason to get all worked up. There's an easy fix."

"What is it?"

He came forward and sat at the edge of my bed. "You just need to sign a pledge of loyalty for me. That will void any right he has."

"Why is this just now coming up? Why didn't he do this before?"

"He didn't know you were half Fae."

"How is that possible? Wouldn't they somehow sense it?"

"No, so someone leaked the info to him."

"Who?"

"I don't know, but I'll handle it when I find out."

"I'm not signing my life over to you."

He stood slowly then turned to face me. "Then there isn't much I can do. I'd pack up your stuff. He's coming tonight." He stood up and started toward the door.

"Are you kidding? You freaked out, made me stay here and had men tailing me to avoid Vitor getting his hands on me. Now you're just going to hand me over? Why didn't you just do it when he was here then?"

"I was trying to give you the courtesy of choosing. I can't legally withhold you." He walked out the door and shut it.

He was bluffing. I threw on a pair of jeans. I'd give him the day to break. He wouldn't just hand me over. No way. I was sure of it. It was true that he wanted to keep me away from the portal, more because he was a control freak than any other reason, in my opinion, but he wouldn't want my abilities in Vitor's hands. I'd play this out and he'd fold like a cheap suit.

Ten hours later, I wasn't so confident anymore. I'd spent the day dawdling around, staying in the penthouse, giving him plenty of opportunity. Nothing, not a peep. I'd even packed up my stuff in my new luggage, supplied by him, and rolled it into the hallway near the door. Still nothing. I was starting to sweat this one out a bit.

Going with Vitor wasn't an option. I didn't even really want to stay here, let alone go there, but now I felt like I had a purpose. I haven't always lived the most moral life. I'd never gone out of my way to be a do-gooder, and I didn't know if I believed in god. If he did exist, I was pretty sure he either didn't know who I was, or just didn't cared. But, something had started to change. I was beginning to feel like I had a purpose that was bigger than me, and I was surprised by how much it was starting to effect my decisions.

Then, there was the page. I couldn't stop from wondering if it somehow was about me. If it was, then that meant Cormac stood for the right.

"Vitor is on his way up," Cormac said as he walked into the living room and disturbed my thoughts.

"Okay." I remained reclined on the couch. He was faking.

A few minutes later, when a knock sounded at the door, I figured it would be Dodd or Buzz joining in the charade.

"Do you want to answer it?" Cormac asked me.

"Sure, it is for me, after all." I walked into the foyer and looked into the peephole to see Vitor standing there. A list of curses ran off in my head.

I walked back into the living room to see that Cormac had taken my spot, reclining upon the couch.

"Fine. What happens if I sign the paper? What

exactly does it entail?"

"It means you are with me. You owe me your loyalty."

"Until when? Forever?"

"No, only until we mutually dissolve it. If you don't, he's going to stalk your every move."

Something about this was bothering me deeply. I was missing something obvious, but Vitor was now pounding on the door in the background and it muddled my thoughts.

"Give it to me."

"You sure?"

"Cormac!" Vitor screamed from the hallway.

"Give it to me."

He walked into his office and I followed him.

He handed me a paper as I grabbed a random pen from the table.

"No, use this."

I took the preferred pen and signed my name in scrolling red. A static charge shocked me when I laid the pen down on the paper.

"I'll go break the news to Vitor. You might want to wait here."

I stood and followed him.

"Or not." He laughed as he paused at the door and waited for me. "So what made you finally decide to choose sides?"

"Did I have another choice?"

"You could've taken your chances with Vitor."

"You mean the alien that is currently banging on the door like a mad man? I figured I'd be better off with a native Earth being." I didn't tell him about eternally blooming lilies or any nonsense of him standing for the "right". I felt like a nut even thinking it, so I certainly wasn't going to say it out loud.

He laid his hand on my shoulder as we approached the foyer and stepped in front of me.

The door swung open and a visibly relieved Vitor stood there staring at me. "Josephine."

"Hi, Vitor."

"We've got a lot to discuss."

Cormac took that time to clear his throat and draw attention to him. "Not as much as you think."

"What are you talking about?"

"Check it out for yourself."

I looked from Cormac to Vitor, wondering what the hell he was talking about. Check out what? A strange look appeared on Vitor's face.

"You had no right!" Vitor suddenly exploded.

I'd never believed Vitor could have been capable of this kind of rage unless I'd seen it.

"Yes, I did. She was willing. I had every right." Cormac leaned against the wall looking bored.

Two things happened then, so fast I could barely keep track. Vitor lunged toward me and Cormac was in front of me blocking his path.

"Try it," Cormac said, and he meant it. He

wanted to rip Vitor to shreds.

I stepped to the side. Cormac stepped with me so I had to settle for the limited view of only seeing half of Vitor's face.

"I think it's time for you to leave now."

Vitor looked close to exploding but he said nothing, just left. As he exited, Cormac signaled outside the door and men I'd never have noticed appeared.

"Vitor is no longer welcome on this level. From now on, if he needs me, he can wait in the downstairs lounge until I'm available." Cormac's men silently nodded and he shut the door.

"Can I see that? I thought it might be a good idea to look at what I signed now that I can't do anything about it."

He handed me the paper that was still in his hand.

"What is this made out of?" I fingered the page for a moment. It felt the same weird way the page I'd gotten from the priest felt.

"It's vellum, calf skin."

"You keep this stuff around for all your letters?"

"Only the contracts and important documents."

"Is that an Alchemist thing?"

"No, it's commonly used by the Fae as well. I'm not sure if it's calf skin in that instance, as I'm not familiar with their livestock, but it's something similar."

I nodded, storing that little tidbit away. I looked over the document, now, for the first real time and realized it wasn't in English. It wasn't in Spanish or French either for that matter. The whole document in numbers.

"This is gibberish."

"Only if you don't know how to read it. It's an ancient Alchemist language."

"Which you know how to write?"

"Yes."

"So what exactly does this say?"

"It just says you're with me."

I looked over the long contract. "There's an awful lot of writing here to say 'you're with me'."

"It's nothing unusual. These documents are very common." He reached over and took the vellum paper from my hand, and I couldn't help but breathe him in. Why did he always smell so damn good? I was relieved when he stepped away and walked back to his office. He took the paper over to a safe hidden behind a wall panel.

"Really? It's worthy of the safe?"

"Just habit," he said, but I wasn't sure I believed him.

"I didn't sign over my first born did I?"

"No. How are you feeling, by the way?"

I turned, watching the Vegas skyline through

the windows, and heard the click of the safe tumblers behind me. He came and perched on the edge of his desk, partially blocking my view of the skyline. I wished it annoyed me but it didn't. He was a gloriously masculine looking man, his shirt sleeves rolled up to his elbows, the fabric stretched tight over his arms as he leaned forward slightly.

"I'm fine. I slept better than I have in ages."

"Yes, that's one of the perks. You sleep like a babe after a nice dose."

"Why aren't you yelling, anymore?"

"I understand why you did it. I'm not mad. I'm just concerned."

I saw a shadow cross his face and he got up quickly, hiding whatever emotion was there. He walked over to the window and watched the same view I'd been admiring. I stood and walked over to stand next to him.

He looked at me and then back out the window. "It never gets dull. You would think, after all this time, I'd be sick of looking at it, but I don't. It's the life and energy. It saturates the air."

"Are you going to let me help again?"

"No."

"Why? It went off perfectly."

"No."

"You make no sense. You wanted me here to help. You wanted me here to keep me from Vitor. Now you almost let Vitor drag me away and you won't let me help. What is your angle?"

He looked down at me and I met his eyes, the lights of the strip reflected upon their icy surface. "I don't need your help at the moment. If it comes to it, I'll reassess then." Then he smirked. "And I was never going to let Vitor have you."

"You were bluffing." I just shook my head annoyed. "God damn it."

"Of course I was bluffing. I own a casino. If I couldn't bluff out a green girl like you, I'd have to sell and walk out with my tail between my legs."

"There's nothing green about me." It wasn't a confessional, just the truth.

"Compared to me, you're as green as spring grass after a week of rain."

"Festiva is in a few days," he said after a long pause. "Did you have any interest in going? We hold it out in the middle of the desert. It's quite an event."

"I didn't know I was invited."

"Because of what you are, you have an automatic invite. It might be a good idea to go, meet all the players on the scene."

"Is it out in the middle of the wide open desert?" Wide open sky above? Uh oh.

"We set up huge tents, but in essence, yes."

Tents, that was good. I couldn't fly off with a tent. "I'll go."

"It's formal. I'll have a driver take us in."

Did I just agree to a date? I wasn't quite sure what I just said yes to, but that last part sounded like a date. He left the room before I could ask. Right, like I would've asked.

Chapter Twenty-One

I'd shopped for days. The way I figured, whatever this was, I needed to look spectacular. It was no secret, most men were easier to manipulate when you looked your best. It went way beyond Cormac tonight. This was my opportunity to get information, and I had a whole lot of questions that still needed answering.

I'd told no one about the bloody scene with my mother twenty years ago, or the crazy page left behind, and I still wasn't going to tell anyone. I also had my own personal stake in what was messing up the portal. I'd tried to broach the subject again with Cormac about getting more involved, but he was putting up a brick wall ever since I'd brought all the people over behind his back. Pleasant, he'd been. Helpful? Not at all. Tonight was going to be all about reconnaissance.

Someone was messing with the portal, and maybe, just maybe, there was a connection between my mother's attack and what was happening now. If that page was about me, there definitely was. I understood the motives for messing with the portal. Now I needed to figure out what had motivated the attack all those years ago. I was becoming increasingly worried. I didn't want to be "the last hope of the bereft" but it was looking like that was exactly who I might be. This just sucked. Who in their right mind would want to be the savior of the bereft? Why couldn't I have turned out to be some long lost Princess of the Rich and Beautiful?

I looked at my reflection one last time. Even with all the hours I'd spent inside lately, my skin still retained its golden glow. My long, naturally blond hair hung almost to my waist in soft platinum waves. The black dress I wore fell quite a bit short of my knees, but not quite high enough to look trashy. It hugged my curves just enough to emphasize my curvy figure without showing every detail. It was the perfect balance of enough, but not too much. I knew I looked my best, and I planned on using it for whatever it was worth tonight.

I guessed there would be alcohol. It was hard to imagine this group having a dry party. In my experience, nothing loosened the lips as much as a few too many drinks. My game plan was to stake out the bar for the drinkers. They were soft targets.

"Are you ready?" I heard Cormac shout from the foyer. A scream from the foyer was not exactly romantic date material. I guess this was business.

"Coming!" I screamed back just as unromantically and put some extra gloss on my lips. Guys loved full glossy lips. I grabbed my dress purse and headed out.

Cormac was standing and looking at his watch when I walked into the foyer, and I was grateful for the few seconds that bought me to hide my reaction. He was in a full tuxedo. I'd never seen a man look sexier in my life. He was primal sex incarnate. It made me resent that this wasn't a date. I had to remember why I'd turned him down in the first place. I couldn't go there. No matter how kind he could be, he was dangerous. I couldn't forget that, but sometimes it was so hard to remember.

He turned his gorgeous pale blue eyes on me. I watched as they ran the length of my body, from my toes to my hair. His eyes stopped on my own with a piercing gaze. It made me remember what his hands felt like, how hot it had been when he'd pressed against me in the elevator.

"Let's go," he said and abruptly broke the eye contact.

There was a stretch limo waiting for us outside. I found it empty when I climbed into the back.

"Where are the guys?"

"They had things to handle over there, so they left before us."

We settled in and rode through the desert in silence. I was used to the silence with him, but the tension was unusually high for a reason I couldn't quite understand.

It broke the moment the lights started to appear in the distance, or perhaps my excitement made me numb to it. In the middle of nothing, Festiva shone like a beacon. Problem was I wasn't sure if it would turn out to be a wealth of information and contacts, or a snake pit. I was more inclined to think it would be of the reptilian variety.

"It's massive."

"Yes, between the people here, and the people that come over for the celebration, it's quite large."

"What are we celebrating again?"

"The signing of the contract and the pact."

"So it was that big of a deal?"

"It was the beginning of everything."

The closer we got the more details I could make out. A glimmering gold fabric tented the massive area and reflected the light of the surrounding torches that lined its perimeter. As we pulled up, I saw just how massive it was. Hundreds of people had attended.

Cormac held out his hand to me as I took a step onto the carpeting that covered the sand. As I got a better look, I ran a self-conscious hand over my dress. These people screamed power and money. I wasn't an insecure person by nature, but I knew when I was outclassed. It might have been the way they stood, or the clothes they wore. I

213

didn't know if I could describe the atmosphere to anyone not there, but it was beyond daunting.

I ran through the speech I'd given myself countless times in my life, the speech I hadn't used in years. I'm just as good as these people. The only difference is consequence of birth. They are no better than I am. It was amazing, no matter how far I came I could be yanked back into that insecure little girl's brain this quickly. Even with a beautiful and expensive dress on, I felt like it was the first day of third grade again, with my hand-me-down clothes.

But, it wasn't third grade, and I wasn't her, anymore. I straightened my spine and strolled into the party as if I owned it. It didn't matter what I felt like on the inside, on the outside I looked calm and cool.

With Cormac by my side, every pair of eyes in the place turned toward us as we made our way through the elaborately decorated area. Lights hung from the top of the tent frames, fountains flowed in every corner. In the center, flame-throwers performed underneath a crystal chandelier, while Arabian looking women danced provocatively.

Cormac grabbed two champagnes from a passing waiter and then started a long procession of introductions, as it seemed that everyone there wanted to meet me. I wasn't sure why I ranked so high, but I barely had a moment to contemplate it as wave after wave approached.

"Why is everyone so interested in me?" I asked Cormac the second there was a break.

"They might have heard things."

"What things?"

"That little trick you pulled in the portal was unusual. They think you have power, and these people like power."

It startled me a little to think that I might have something everyone else wanted. It wasn't a position I was used to being in. I scanned the crowd, wondering if I could use this to my advantage.

"Are you all right? You look a touch flushed."

"I'm fine, but I am going to step outside. I need some air. It's pretty packed in here."

"If you give me a minute, I can go with you, but I have to check on a couple of things first."

"Since when did I become someone you needed to tend?" I wanted to bite my tongue the second I said it. I knew why I did it. No matter whether I wanted to or not, regardless of what had transpired between us, I liked him, and I didn't want to.

"Fine," he said as he walked away. The words were mild, but the tone held an edge.

It didn't matter. After I got my answers, and he got his portal issue fixed, I would be leaving.

This was a short-term situation. I couldn't afford emotional entanglements with these people. If I decided to start laying roots, this wasn't the garden I had in mind.

I stepped away quickly, before I was cornered by anyone else. It was nice to be away from the crowd, getting a breather. I'd never excelled at small talk, and for all that these people weren't exactly people, they sure liked their small talk.

Once I was outside, I was too nervous to step far from the tent, and made sure I stayed within reach of it, just in case I started floating or something else odd. Hidden in the shadows, I was safely out of site when I heard Tracker speaking to someone, not even ten feet away.

"What the fuck happened?"

"It wasn't my fault. It was her."

"I've about had it. You need to fix this. We've lost all the progress we've made."

"I'll handle it."

"You'd better. Come on, I don't want to talk here."

I watched the two men cross the distance to enter the tent opening. They had to be talking about the portal. I rushed back into the tent, and scanned the heads for Cormac's. He was across the room, but it took me forever to get there, with every third person stopping me to talk.

When I finally got within reach of him, he was

talking to someone I couldn't see. I tapped his back to get his attention, as it was such a close press, it was hard to circle around.

When he turned toward me, I lost my voice. Lacey stood in front of him, looking up at him doe eyed. I was friends with Lacey. She was a good person. So why did I want to rip her eyes out when I saw her staring at him like that?

"Jo!" she greeted me excitedly, and made me feel that much worse for my reaction to seeing her. "Cormac just told me you were here."

Cormac? When did these two get on a first name basis?

"What are you doing here?"

"Cormac asked me if I wanted to work it."

It wasn't until that minute that I realized she was in a server outfit. It would've appeased my newly jealous nature, except their body language told a different story. If they weren't sleeping together now, they might be soon. They stood shoulder to shoulder facing me. I stood alone. You ever want to know who's with whom in a party; that was as clear as body language could get.

"Everything okay?"

My need to tell him about Tracker's suspicious conversation fell from my brain, as I grappled for something calm to discuss.

"Hello, everyone." I heard Vitor's voice come up at my side. All annoyance at the stunt he had

217

tried to pull disappeared, as he leaned down and kissed my cheek.

"Vitor, it's nice to see you." He all of a sudden became my life raft, as I felt emotionally swept down the river.

"Yes, Vitor, it's great to see you." The acid in Cormac's voice wasn't hidden. I turned to see Cormac's gaze eyeing my hand that was now resting on Vitor's arm. I wasn't even aware I had grasped him until that moment. Cormac's hand then disappeared to rest on the small of Lacey's back, and I saw the hope flare in her large eyes as he did it.

I was annoyed with him for leading her on, but she wasn't stupid. She only believed what she wanted. Nothing I could say to her would warn her off, not when she was so clearly infatuated. It made me angry with him for using her, and angry with her for no reason at all, or not one I'd thought up yet.

"Would you like to get a drink with me?" Vitor asked perceptively.

"Sure," I replied to Vitor. "Have fun," I tossed back to them over my shoulder.

I felt Cormac's gaze on my back, as Vitor parted the crowd for us as we made our way across the expanse.

"Why are there humans working this? Isn't that risky?"

218

"No, we always have them. Normally nothing happens that would raise alarm. If it does, we handle it," Vitor explained.

I knew exactly how they handled it and I fought the urge to find Lacey and drag her out of there. That might be enough reason on its own.

"I'm glad we have a moment. I really wanted to speak with you about the other day."

"You acted crazy," I told him. Now that I had some space from Cormac, my brain was remembering just how annoyed I had been with Vitor.

"I'm sorry. I was upset because I know you would be safer and more comfortable among us."

"You should have made an offer, instead of trying to force the issue." We stopped at one of the various bars set up in the corner, slightly tucked away, and I asked the bartender for a shot of tequila. Vitor signaled for him to bring two.

"I tried; I've been looking for you ever since I found out."

"Why don't we just talk straight? You want me to help you operate the portal, and if I wanted to help you, I would have. Don't ever try to force my hand, again."

"Yes, you're right. I did want your help, but once I found out you were of our clan, I was honestly trying to look out for your best interests."

"I don't need you to. How did you find out I

had Fae blood, anyway?"

"Let's just leave it at: I've got some connections."

"It doesn't matter. The point is I resent you interfering."

"I know you are tied to him now. I'm sorry if my actions contributed to that."

"You never know what will happen when you back someone into a corner." I threw my shot back and felt the burn trail down my throat.

"I would undo it if I could."

"No need." I didn't hate him, in all honesty I liked Vitor. I wasn't sure why, but something in my gut said he was decent guy, whether I admitted it to him or not. But, he'd screwed up my situation even worse, and that was saying something.

From that point forward, the night dragged on at an unforgiving pace. I felt like I was a zombie giving obligatory replies to mindless questions. As distracted as I was, I still couldn't keep my eyes from wandering, tracking Cormac across the room, and all too often I'd spot Lacey not far away.

I still needed to talk to him, though. Tracker had a hand in whatever was going wrong. The sooner this whole mess got sorted out, the sooner I could leave.

Chapter Twenty-Two

I stumbled through the penthouse the next day, more than slightly hung over. At some point last night, without meaning to, I'd had one too many tequilas.

"Cormac!" I held my hand to my forehead and moaned. I needed to keep my own voice down.

"I'm in here."

I slogged along toward his bedroom. As I entered, he walked out of his bathroom, just freshly showered with a towel slung low on his hips. God, life was so unfair sometimes.

"What did you need?"

He just stood there, one towel away from naked, his skin tan and glistening. I forced myself to look only at his eyes and refused to ask him to get dressed. Way too obvious.

"I want to talk to you about Tracker."

"What about him?"

"I think he's behind the problems with the portal."

"I've considered it, but no, I don't think so." He walked over to his closet, pulling out a pair of slacks and a dress shirt and laid them on the bed. The idea he might start dressing while I stood there sent me into a near panic, and I started babbling off the conversation I had overheard outside the

221

tent last night to him, and watched his profile for a reaction.

"Remember when you brought over that kid the first time?" He stopped fiddling with his clothes and half sat on his night table, his towel hanging precariously.

"How could I forget?"

"I'd felt a disturbance then. Whatever has been going wrong was still in play that night. That kid was Tracker's baby brother. Tracker wouldn't hurt him in a million years. A lot of things are debatable, but he loves that kid."

"Well, then, who do you think it is?"

"I think it's Vitor."

"No. It's not Vitor."

"And you know this because of the handful of times you've met him?"

"It's not him. I know he's desperate to bring his people over, and I'm not saying he's completely innocent, but I don't think it's him."

His towel still hung on as he crossed the floor toward me, and stopped close enough that I could smell the heady masculine scent of him.

"What do you have going on with him?"

"Nothing. What do you have going on with Lacey?" I had to force my eyes to stay on his face.

"Did that bother you?"

"Not at all, I just thought we were onto the portion of the conversation where we discussed our personal involvements."

"So you do have a thing for Vitor?" His tone was an octave lower when he asked.

A warning pricked at my senses but I still said, "God, you're thick headed sometimes. Just stay away from Lacey. I don't want her messed up in all this."

"She's a grown woman, she can make her own choices."

It was time to make my exit before things got heated, one way or another. As I walked back to my room, all I could think of was, he was wrong. Well, that wasn't the only thing I could think of, but it was the only thought I was willing to admit. Tracker had something to do with this, and if Cormac wasn't going to listen, I'd handle it on my own.

Decided in my new course of action, it was around noon when I hit the casino floor, showered and dressed. First stop, Jonny. What they say about bartenders always knowing the comings and goings had more than a grain of truth in it.

"Where have you been?" he asked me when I found him carrying out bottles to stock the bar.

"I took some time off, family issues."

"Really? I heard you were shacked up with Cormac."

"I'm not shacked up with him." The pout that appeared on his face told me I shouldn't have decided to be so forthcoming, all of a sudden. When had I ever had an aversion to lying?

"It certainly looks like it. Especially now that I hear you're living with him." His voice held a slight edge and I wondered just how deep his crush was.

"It's a long story. Have you seen Tracker?"

"Tracker? What do you want with him? Didn't you guys get off on a bad foot, or are you looking to date him now, too?"

"No, I'm not and yes, we did, but I wanted to talk to him. Have you seen him? Jonny, please don't give me a hard time. I really can't deal with it right now."

"He's walking off the floor behind you," he said, while he tilted his head in the direction he meant.

I snapped my head around and saw that same ugly red leather jacket, as I watched him walk out the entrance. I really did hate that jacket.

"Thanks, Jonny!" I thought I heard him ask me something, but I'd already started to walk after Tracker as quickly as I could, without drawing attention to myself. I paused at the entrance. If he had turned right, it would have led him into the Lacard mall, left led to the main entrance and the Vegas Strip. I spotted him walking out onto the Vegas Strip and I froze.

Other than Festiva, I hadn't ventured outside in weeks, ever since I had awoken stuck to the ceiling. I'd made excuses for why I hadn't needed to. How the Lacard was its own contained world. Who needed to go outside? Nothing out there but the world right? But there was no more stalling. I'd have to get over this, or be stuck here indefinitely. I'd never be able to prove my case against Tracker if I couldn't even get up the nerve to leave the building.

As I stood there thinking, I knew he was getting farther and farther away. That's it, I wasn't a coward, get yourself together I told myself. Dodd had been right, I wasn't really that afraid of death, but I was terrified of heights. That's what made it even more ridiculous. If I started to float, it wasn't the possible plummet to the ground that scared the shit out of me, but the view before I crashed.

I yanked the baseball cap from my back pocket, shoved my hair up underneath it and lowered my sunglasses onto my face. Admittedly, it wasn't the best disguise ever, but if I kept my distance it could work.

As I followed him the couple of blocks over to the Bellagio, the Lacards toughest competition, I stayed close to anything I thought I could grab onto in case I started floating. He didn't go in, just paused by the fountain while the water show played. The water did its dance to an Italian opera classic that I recognized but couldn't name.

He was fidgety and repeatedly scanned the

crowd. When his eyes darted my way, I ducked behind a group taking pictures, pretty confident he hadn't seen me. Oh yes, he was looking for someone. Could this P.I. stuff really be this simple? Just tail and wait? Those guys got paid too much.

Tracker's eyes land on a middle-aged guy in a dark suit, he scanned the area again, but returned his gaze right back to the guy. I pulled out my phone and snapped a couple of shots of the man he watched, but then the guy walked right past him. When Tracker didn't move for a couple of minutes, I started to wonder if I was wrong.

Suddenly, Tracker took off in the same direction. I followed Tracker, who followed the guy for another few minutes. The guy unexpectedly ducked into one of those quickie medical clinics. Tracker followed less than five minutes later and I knew I was on to something. Tucking myself into a dark corner, I got comfortable to wait it out.

"Cormac is looking for you." I yelped, as Dodd's voice startled me twenty minutes later.

"Did you follow me? I thought we were done with that stuff?"

"I didn't follow you. Cormac told me where you were."

"How did he know?"

He just raised his eyebrows and threw his hands up in the air.

"What does he want?"

"No clue."

I weighed my decision. I would surely be spotted if I stayed here, and Dodd wouldn't leave easily. Better to take the knowledge I had than blow my cover. Tracker might try to cover his movements better if he knew I was watching him.

"Let's go." I shot past him and sprinted from one large object to the next large object.

"What's the rush? And why does it look like any moment you are going to hug a building or a bench?"

I put my arm through his, figuring he was a decent anchor, and I slowed suddenly. "No rush. Want to stop for a latte on the way back?"

He looked down at me oddly. "Are you hitting on me?"

"No, what a bizarre thing to ask."

"Yes, I'm the one acting bizarre."

"Are you going to get a latte with me, or not?"

"Sure."

"So, what's the status with you and Cormac? Was he really pissed off at you after you and I ran the portal?"

"I thought he was going to knock me out. Thank god, he didn't figure out the lead was fake."

"Is that normal for you guys? Hitting each other?"

"No, but that's how pissed he was. He got over it, though."

"When I didn't see you around for a couple, I was wondering."

"What he do to you?"

"Nothing, really, other than I'm banned from anything to do with the portal."

"That's not good. How we going to get all these people back?"

"He's going to have to cave."

"I don't know about that."

"Maybe since we did it last time with no problems, he'll be a bit more relaxed. Plus, I signed some sort of fealty contract you guys have. That should make him feel more secure, right?"

"What did you sign?"

"That fealty contract. You know what I'm talking about, right? I thought it was standard?"

"Oh, yeah, that. It's been so long I forgot about it."

"So, then, it's normal?" I asked, looking for a little more reassurance now that his reaction had been so strange.

"Completely, don't worry about it." The noise and proximity of the people in the crowded coffee house effectively stopped our conversation.

Chapter Twenty-Three

"What's going on?" I asked as I walked into the penthouse. Cormac was leaning over a table as he peered at papers splayed out in front of him.

"Have a seat." He still hadn't looked up at me.

Oh, god, this wasn't going to be a good conversation. Great, what was his problem?

He finally straightened out and rubbed the back of his neck. He looked over at me, let out a sigh, and just shook his head.

"Let me start by saying that this does not change my opinion on your earlier actions," he said.

I watched him walk over and sit on the couch opposite me. Normally, he stood when he talked. He'd walk over to the window and watch the skyline or walk to the bar. He didn't sit that often and when he had, I never liked what he had to say. And if he did sit, he would lean forward, ready to pounce at any moment. He didn't lean back and recline the way he was now.

"Unfortunately, I can't see any way around it. I'm going to need you to get in the portal when we operate it again, like you did last time." He leaned his head against the back of the sofa facing the ceiling, eyes closed.

Knowing he couldn't see me, I didn't try to

temper the gloating smile. I wasn't sure I could. Mr. Know It All just had to admit he needed me. This was definitely going to buy me some leverage.

"Well?" he said. "Let's hear it."

"I want my own place while I'm here."

"No."

"Why not?"

"I took off the tail. That will have to be enough."

"Who cares if you took off the tail? You seem to know my every movement anyway. And how exactly is that?"

"I can't disclose that information. But, once I dissolve the second contract you signed, that will end. How about a trust in your name?"

"How much?"

"Five hundred thousand. It will pay for all your student loans. You would have a fresh start after this is done."

The idea made me want to do cartwheels, but I wasn't going to admit it. If I verbally relented, god knows what else he'd try to gain. If you gave Cormac an inch, he took a football field.

"Agreed. What's the deal with the portal? Still no idea what's going wrong?"

He ran his hand through his hair, and I knew the answer before he even said the word no.

"The only thing I can figure out is that they must have one or more of us pulling the radiation from the other side. Pulling just enough that it offsets our force and stalls in the portal. That's why what you did was so effective. I'm still mad that you did it. You had no idea whether it would work or not, but it seems to be the only option right now."

"I agree. So what's the plan?"

"You are now officially on the team. But, I want to be there every time. No exceptions. I'm still not completely comfortable with this. I think that whoever is behind this, is going to try a different tactic, soon. When they can't shut it down one way, they'll try another. I don't want you to get stuck in the crossfire."

"When I was out, I happened to notice Tracker."

"You just happened to notice him?"

"Yes, it was a pure coincidence."

He rolled his eyes but didn't say anything else.

"So, like I was saying, I noticed Tracker, and I think he was meeting with another man. It seemed shady."

"Well? What happened exactly?"

"It looked like he followed him into a doctor's office."

"I don't want you following him again."

"I wasn't following him today."

"Don't do it again. He's dangerous."

"I can handle him."

"Why are you so goddamn stubborn? What happened to 'it's not my problem'?"

"That was before I realized how much you and these people were going to mess up my world." As I said the words, I realized how true they were. This was my problem. I couldn't walk away, even if I wanted to, not when I knew the consequences. My whole life I had been about what was best for Jo, and this was when I had to decide to be a bigger person? Had my conscience simply been waiting for the biggest cluster fuck it could find?

"I'm going to handle it."

"Whatever, Boss." I dropped the subject. I had no desire to argue with him about an order I had no intention of following.

We sat in silence for a while before I decided to broach the next subject. "I saw a picture of your father once. It was in an article about how he started a real estate business that you grew and eventually used to fund building this casino. He was in his thirties in the picture. You looked just like him."

"Yes, I did. He's passed on now."

"I saw that. I'm sorry."

"As to that matter, I've got a few people working on yours, but they've been coming up dry. Is there anything you remember at all that might give them a lead?"

"No." I'd said it too quickly. Just call me

Captain Obvious why don't you.

"I don't know what secrets you're holding on to, but maybe it could help. If you want this information, I would think you would want to tell them."

"It's not important."

"You don't know that. If you want to find them, you need to give us everything you have."

"I'm doing my end, you do yours. I'm not obligated to hand over every little nitty-gritty detail of my life to you."

"Really? Every nitty-gritty detail? Your life is a whopping black hole!"

"This conversation is over." I got off the couch before he could continue but I didn't make it out of the room in time to miss his last comment.

"Go ahead, Jo. Just keep running."

I slammed my door in response. He didn't know me.

Chapter Twenty-Four

"Why am I getting calls that you've been standing here all day?"

I turned to look at Cormac over the rim of my cup as I sipped my latte. "I haven't been here all day. You should tell your spies to be more accurate."

"You've been here a while."

"I like watching the people."

"Why watch them through the glass? Why don't you go outside and sit on the bench, since you are becoming such a people person?"

"I'm happy right where I am."

"Dodd told me you were acting kind of funny the other day."

"Do you know every single thing I do?"

He nodded. "Come with me."

"Where?"

"You'll like it."

I followed him up to the penthouse hallway, but instead of making a right, we made a left. He opened a door on the opposite end and I stepped in as he flicked the lights on. A staircase loomed in front of me but we were already on the top floor. And then it clicked. The roof.

"I completely forgot, I've got something I was supposed to do."

I bolted toward the door but he stood in front and blocked my way. "You can do this."

I dropped all pretenses. The gig was up. "No, I can't. I really, really can't."

"You have to get past this."

"Nope, I don't think so. This place is really quite large. I can do everything I need to here."

"Listen to me, if this was a phobia of something stupid, like snakes, we could work with it, no big deal. Even if it was a fear of something stupid, like, milk. Still not a big deal." He grabbed my shoulders and angled my face towards his. "Jo, you won't go outside. We can't just avoid this!"

"I think I can."

"I know you like to run."

"You have a gym. You've really done quite well planning this place out. I have no reason to leave."

"So you are agreeing to live here, forever?"

"You know what? You suck," I said and plopped down on the stairs. I wouldn't go up and I couldn't go out.

He sat down next to me and I was extremely conscious of his side grazing mine.

"We have to do this."

I didn't say anything, just rested my forehead on my knees.

"Jo, you know I'm right."

"I'm scared." I didn't look up.

235

"I've been thinking a lot about what happened that night. I think you've been repressing your abilities so much that when you sleep is the only time your subconscious can let loose a bit."

"I was stuck. What if that happens outside?"

"I think you got stuck because you woke up and panicked. Your subconscious didn't realize it was feeling the ceiling. It thought you were stuck to the floor."

"What if you are wrong?" I finally lifted my head to look at him.

"Let's try. I promise I'll hold onto you the entire time, unless you tell me to let go." He held out his hand to me and I took it. It reminded me of another time he had held out his hand to me and I'd hesitated. I was starting to trust him.

I climbed the stairs to the roof with leaden feet.

"It's going to be okay."

I nodded but I was sick.

When he opened the door, I was awestruck. I expected to see a plain roof with a lousy tar floor. What I got was a nighttime wonderland.

Real grass covered the ground; a pool glistened in the center, with lights glowing all along a glass enclosure that ran the perimeter of the roof. Full-grown citrus trees grew next to arbors and stone pathways led to wrought iron chairs. It was magical.

The sound of Desert Rose by Sting filled the air. As we walked forward, I half expected a wood nymph to spring out in front of me.

"This is my favorite spot," he said as we stopped about ten feet from the edge of the roof with its magnificent view. There were two giant weeping willows trimmed in such a way as to create an alcove, and clumps of wild flowers lay at our feet.

"How is this possible?"

"The trees?"

"Everything."

"I'm the only one on the floor beneath. A huge chunk of it is taken up by the pool and the tree root systems."

"It's incredible."

"I'm glad you like it."

I felt his hand pull from mine but my panic was short lived as I felt his hand come around my back. He guided my other hand to his shoulder.

"I don't dance."

He pulled me into a soft embrace and started to move to the music. "Relax. We're just friends hanging out on a rooftop."

I started to move with him as I looked everywhere but his face. It was almost too easy. Our body's fit together perfectly as we moved in sync. I could feel his heat surround me as we danced in a magical garden with the lights of Vegas

237

around us.

When I finally looked up at him, I knew what I'd been avoiding. Even when he was relaxed as he was now, his intensity drew me. When I looked into his eyes, I felt laid bare. As if he could see right to the core of me. It drew me in as much as it frightened me.

I raised my face to his. Right now, I didn't care what might come of us, I just wanted to feel him. I saw understanding in his eyes but instead of meeting me, he pulled back, and my world shifted on its axis. Had he just rejected me?

"How do you feel?"

"Hmmm? I'm fine."

"I'm not holding your hand anymore."

So wrapped up in the moment, everything else had fallen from notice. As I realized I now stood alone, I had to fight the urge not to cling to the closest tree, but I didn't.

"You aren't floating away." He smiled but awkwardness hung in the air. Although nothing was said, we both knew what had just happened.

"Yes, I guess I'm cured. Mostly, anyway."

"It'll take a while to completely get over it."

"Yes." My mind was racing so fast it was hard to even keep track of what he was saying. "I'm actually a little cold. Let's go back in."

As we left the roof, I pondered to myself how quickly things change. The pursued to the rejected,

238

and what a bitter taste it left.

Chapter Twenty-Five

While I cleaned out my trailer fridge, I thought of the last visitors from Festiva who had left this morning. I hadn't been here in a while, and although I was about as far from Susie homemaker as you got, the milk and few other provisions I did have were long past their prime.

I'd come over here this morning to pay the rent for the next three months—working for Cormac paid generously. I also needed some space. It was hard getting use to this much togetherness, especially with how rejected I felt. I needed somewhere private to lick my wounds. I wasn't used to having people around constantly. If it wasn't Cormac, it was Dodd or Buzz. Then there was Ben. I don't know where he had gone for the last week but he was there all the time, now.

I couldn't even leave without the Cormac interrogation of where I was headed, another thing that drove me crazy, lately. I wanted to walk out the door for once without everyone having to know where I was going, and what I was doing. When I told him I was headed here, he couldn't understand why. It was perhaps the stupidest question he had asked. Eventually this portal issue would be resolved, was I supposed to live in a tent in the desert, then? I knew he figured I'd have the

240

money, but maybe I didn't want to blow it on a place I didn't need. Maybe I liked my trailer, even if no one else did.

It had been a little stressful getting here, since I still had my fear-of-floating-away anxiety going on, but it hadn't happened once while I was awake. Since being on the roof the other night, I was starting to feel confident that maybe I wouldn't drift off into space. I guess there was one positive thing that came out of it.

Walking around my little space, I was so glad I'd come. I lounged on my couch and flipped on my crappy little TV. It was a second hand couch, I stared at a twenty-inch screen, and I was happy. The setting sun filtered in a warm glow through my window, and I completely relaxed for the first time in weeks.

I heard my phone ring in my purse, and I wanted to ignore it. Only Cormac and his men called me. I wanted, no needed, a Cormac free zone, but I knew if I didn't answer, I'd most likely have someone pounding on the door, soon. I gave up and dug my phone out.

"Hello?"

"Where are you?"

"I'm at my place, Cormac. I told you I would be here."

"When are you coming back?"

"I'm staying here for tonight," I said and then

waited.

"Okay. When you coming back?"

I would have fallen over if I hadn't been sitting. No fight?

"I'll be back at nine."

No argument, he just hung up. That was easy. Perhaps I was toeing the line too much. Nah, that couldn't be it.

I looked out the window, knowing that there wasn't much time before full nightfall, and quickly grabbed my worn out sneakers. I hadn't been out running in weeks. I'd gone on the treadmill in the gym of the casino, but I longed to be outside. I wanted to feel my body moving, instead of feeling like a gerbil on a wheel.

I stretched my legs, then ran at a sprint because the world lay open and I could. I pushed all anxiety away, refusing even to think of it. I quickly became winded, and then fell into a slower steady pace. I didn't make my way back to my place until a light sheen of sweat covered me and there was only the tiniest glimmer of light left in the sky.

My panting, and my complete physical relaxation from the strenuous exertion, added to my being oblivious to the two men until one of them had my arm wrenched behind my back.

The other thug, the one I could see, circled in front of me.

"You sure this is her?" He was huge, with a thick barrel chest, and greasy hair.

"She looks identical to the picture," the guy who held me said.

"Okay, let's get her to the car before anyone sees us."

I fell limp, lulling the guy holding me into a false sense of security. I didn't look like a threat, and I didn't want to let them know I might be one. Might, I wasn't sure, myself, how much of one I really was. I saw their car not twenty feet away, and I wanted to shoot myself for not having noticed it before. Didn't matter, as long as these two weren't Keepers, I could take them. I'd prefer the odds of one at a time, hell, I'd prefer a lot of things to be different, but that wasn't working out too hot for me.

The larger of the two men walked ahead, clearly not concerned about me, which left me with just the one in near proximity. I'd never done it blind before, but I shot the energy through my arms, hoping for good contact.

It wasn't perfect, but he let out a yelp and released me long enough to finish the job. My knee connected between his legs and I blasted him full force. Before I'd finished, a hand grabbed my shoulder, and ripped me away from my current victim. With no time to dodge the huge fist aimed right at my face, I concentrated on throwing my

243

hands on his arm when he connected. It hurt like a son of a gun when he did, and I was afraid I'd lose consciousness, but I held on. I'd managed to throw enough juice at him that he was clutching his arm in agony. I wasn't sure how long I'd have, so I took off at a run with no cell phone or purse.

I couldn't find a single pay phone. Ever since cell phones, they've become increasingly harder and harder to find. An hour later, I was still jogging at a steady pace and had just made it to the Vegas Strip. I knew I must have looked a wreck because of the number of stares I received.

I'd given up on stopping to call, and just jogged the whole way over. My legs burned worse than the last marathon I'd run, and I never thought I'd feel so grateful to be back at Lacard.

No one questioned me as I walked in. They all recognized me. I wasn't sure if Cormac handed my picture out or what, but lately I could do whatever I wanted without so much as a raised eyebrow.

My feet were sore by the time I stepped out of the elevator into the hallway that led to the penthouse. The hall was empty, which was slightly unusual, but not unheard of when Cormac was home. You couldn't get off of his floor without entering a code, anyway, so it wasn't necessary.

The moment I opened the door, I knew something was odd. I just didn't know what. Then I noticed the smell of perfume that lingered in the

244

air, and it clawed at my brain. I knew that scent.

I turned the corner to find Lacey's back to me, her hand rested on Cormac's thigh. Cormac's eyes shifted upward to mine instantly and locked.

I wasn't sure what he saw there, but I knew what I felt like. It stabbed right to the heart of me. While I attacked, he'd been trying to screw the only friend I'd ever had.

The other night suddenly made sense to me. He'd moved on. I said nothing, I knew I didn't have any valid cause to be upset. I stepped out of the room before Lacey even noticed my presence, and closed my door as silently as possible. Then I lay on my bed in the dark.

When a knock sounded on my door less than five minutes later, I wasn't sure who it was, Lacey or Cormac. It didn't make a difference. I didn't want to see either of them. Lacey was still the only friend I had and I didn't want to not be happy for her, but it was hard and I needed a little time to adjust. And Cormac, well, I just didn't want to see him.

"I'm just getting in the shower."

"Let me in." It was Cormac's baritone voice.

"I'll come out when I'm done."

My eyes shot to the door as it swung open.

"What the hell happened to you? You're a mess."

I had a vague idea of what I probably looked

245

like. I knew my nose had bled when the thug punched me in the face, I was also aware my torn shirt and who knew how much dirt clung to me.

"How did you get in? Where is Lacey?"

"I sent Lacey home. Told her I forgot about a meeting."

"You never forget anything."

"Yeah, well, she bought it."

"How did you get in?"

"Hanger. Now what happened to you? You're a wreck."

"Two guys jumped me on my way back from a jog." I gave him a complete rundown of the short events.

"Did they say anything else?"

"Nothing much. Just compared me to a photo they had and agreed I was the correct target."

"Let me look at your nose."

"My nose is fine."

"It looks broken."

"Ow! Get off!" I said as he leaned over me and started touching my face.

"We've got to get that set unless you want to look like a former boxer for the rest of your days. I'll call the doctor."

"I'll do it myself."

"You'll never be able to do it yourself."

He reached in again to touch my face and I knocked his hand away.

"Why are you angry?"

"I'm not," I screamed.

I pushed off the bed and stepped around him into the bathroom. My reflection caught me a bit off guard; blood had dripped down my face and made a trail down the front of my ripped shirt. Cormac's reflection over my left shoulder grimaced.

"We have to get that set. Your bones are already meshing together."

"I'm handling it." I gently ran my fingers along the crooked bridge of my nose, trying to determine the best way to proceed.

"You have no right to be mad."

"I'm not sure if you noticed, but I don't have a lot of friends. Do you have to fuck the only one I have?"

"I haven't fucked her. She's a nice girl. Did you want me to wait around forever?"

I didn't want to admit it, but yes, that is exactly what I had wanted him to do. Just because I rejected him, didn't mean he was supposed to move to the next girl. What kind of crap was that?

"Why her?"

"Why not? Did you have someone else in mind?"

Unfortunately, I did, whether I wanted to admit it or not. Not willing to go there, I ignored the question and tried to figure out what to do about my nose. He was right, if I didn't get it straightened out soon, I would indeed look like an ex-boxer. I gripped the bottom portion of my nose and saw Cormac shake his head.

"You're going to do it wrong."

"Shut up. I've got this under control."

I closed my eyes, took a large breath and tried to ram it into place. The pain was horrific and it took a minute to catch my breath and get control. Once I did, I looked at my handy work. It looked worse than when I had started.

"I told you. Now turn around and let me see how much worse you made it."

I complied out of a sheer panic of vanity. I'd always been pretty, and I suddenly realized I didn't want to be any other way.

"We might not have time to call the doctor. You're really starting to set up."

"That quickly?"

"It happens like that sometimes."

"You're right, I can't do it. Fix it."

"It's going to hurt like hell."

"Just do it."

"You sure?"

"I don't want a crooked nose. Do it!"

I thought he was going to argue with me, but he just snapped my bones back. The pain shot through my head and I ran over to the toilet and threw up what little I had eaten.

248

A wet towel hung near my face after I finished.

"I thought you were going to give me a warning first."

"Just makes it worse."

"Not possible. It didn't feel that bad when it happened."

"You had adrenaline pumping through you. I'm putting the guys back on you."

"No, you are not."

"Yes, I am."

"You gave me your word."

"When you weren't being attacked."

"So you are breaking it?"

He stood silently for a moment. I knew I had hit a nerve. "How about no guards as long as you are on the casino grounds? You take someone if you go anywhere else."

I was about to open my mouth in protest.

"Work with me."

"Fine. Now back up. You're crowding me." Every cell in my body was at full alert with him so close.

He didn't move an inch. "Sooner or later, you are going to have to work on this intimacy problem you have. You wonder why I'm interested in Lacey, why I didn't touch you on the rooftop? Because of this."

I looked into his eyes. "Don't you get it? I'm

broken, and not the kind that can be fixed. This is who I am and who I'm always going to be. And I'm sick of hearing you tell me what's wrong, so either deal with it or I'm leaving." His eyes were so intense on me it chilled my skin and I forgot any pain my nose had caused. Unsettled, I folded and moved first, leaving him standing alone in the bathroom as I walked out the door.

"So does that mean you are admitting there is a problem?" I heard him yell as I walked to the other room.

Chapter Twenty-Six

"Maybe we should hold hands like we did with the radiation problem?" I asked as I banged the back of my head against the hard wall that was acting as my seat back.

"No, this part doesn't work like that," Dodd explained.

"Maybe I should jump in it before it slams shut?" I offered.

"Not a chance. It could crush you," said Cormac.

It was almost two in the morning and they still couldn't get the portal up and running for longer than a minute. The two people who were traveling back had been waiting in the other room for four hours now.

"Boss?"

"What's up, Buzz?"

"They're getting pretty impatient over there and Tracker just showed. He wants to know why his people haven't crossed, yet."

"Tell them it's off for tonight. I'll come over and talk to Tracker in a couple of minutes."

I leaned my head back against the wall and closed my eyes. This had just gone from bad to disastrous. I heard the click of the door shutting and opened my eyes just in time to see Dodd's

251

hand slam against the table. Cormac stood deathly still, just staring at where the portal should have hovered open, displaying a beautiful lavender sky.

I stood and stamped the pins and needles out of my foot. "There has to be someone with answers. I can't believe you guys don't have an owner's manual or something."

"I wish," Cormac replied.

"Well, who trained you? You must have had some sort of mentor?"

"That would be Hammond. The guy I can't find. Let me go get this over with." I watched Cormac's heavy steps as he left the room.

"What's he going to say?" I asked Dodd.

"I don't know, but he'll buy us some time. I'll be right back. I'm going to see if I can help things along a little."

"Yeah, go. I'll be here doing nothing."

Alone in the room, I ran my hand down one of the ebony monoliths, wishing I could unlock a problem that people so much more knowledgeable than me were stymied by, and I was frustrated. Knowing the room was soundproofed, I let out a scream that contained all my pent up anger at the situation, my repressed anger at always being the underdog, and most of all, I released my disgust of myself at being helpless.

The lights in the room flickered off, and were quickly replaced by the portal bursting open. I'd never seen it so large in any of the times I'd been there. It shot toward the ceiling and pressed from wall to wall, leaving dents where the walls strained to contain it.

On the other side, I saw two men, one I didn't recognize, but the other was the guy in the suit who had gone into the doctor's office with Tracker. Both of their faces gaped open in shock.

"Who are you?" the man in the suit hollered down the length of the portal.

"Who are you?" I hollered back. Who'd this guy think he was?

He stepped into the portal and started making his way to me.

I didn't want to panic, but I had a real bad feeling about this guy. I considered making a break for the door, but I didn't want to run. Something about the idea of running from this guy made me mad, so I stood my ground.

As long as he wasn't immune to my skills, I could take him. He was about five feet ten inches and of average build. His appearance gave me the impression that he wasn't the type to get physical, or at least, he didn't look like he was used to getting dirty, might be a more accurate way to describe him.

His shoes hitting the interior floor announced his official exit from the portal.

"Who are you?"

His voice was deep, even now that he wasn't yelling. I saw the silver at his temples and slight wrinkling at the corner of his eyes. Even without this display of age, I could sense his experience by his carriage and the confidence he held within himself.

"Not going to answer?" he asked.

"I'm not sure why you think I owe you any answers?"

"It doesn't matter. I might not know what hole you dragged yourself out of, but I know who you are, regardless."

"Excuse me? Would you care to elaborate?"

"You stand there like your tough and confident, but I know the truth that lies beneath the act. Now, it's time you crawl back to the gutter and get out of my business."

"You're right, I do come from the gutter, and guess what? That's how I fight too." Before I gave him even a second to react, I kicked him in the stomach. I threw everything I had into it and he fell backward into the portal. The rage over his words, and my fear that he was correct, fueled my energy as it shot out of me. He'd been so confident in his physical superiority his relaxed posture had made him an easy mark and he flew back a couple feet into the portal.

A second after he hit the portal, I heard the door swing open. As I turned to see Cormac and

Dodd walking in, I felt a swoosh of air as the portal instantly collapsed with a force so strong it created an aftershock that shook the very walls.

"Oh, god!" I said frantically, looking from Dodd to Cormac. "I gotta get this thing back open!"

"What the…"

"Cormac, I just shoved a man in there before it collapsed!"

"What the hell happened in here?" Dodd finally articulated. The two of them circled the room, the smell of dust in the air.

"Whatever you did dented the walls."

I turned to where Cormac stood, and I saw the cracks that were running floor to ceiling. It looked like an explosion had happened.

My hands started to shake violently and I started gasping for air. It felt like I couldn't catch my breath no matter how hard I tried.

"It's okay. Just relax," Cormac said, his arm around me.

"I killed him." I'd done horrible things, but this was a first. I'd hurt people, but I had never, ever, killed a single soul.

"Who?" His hand was rubbing my back, and as much as I wanted to fall into the curve of his arm, I thought of the man's words before he died.

"The guy I saw with Tracker. I killed him. I pushed him into the portal and then it collapsed."

"What did he look like?"

With shaky hands, I reached in and pulled out my phone, flipping through the pictures.

"This is him." I handed my phone to Cormac, Dodd looking over his shoulder.

"I can't make out anything. It's a complete blur."

"It's not like I could ask him to stand still and pose."

"Can you make anything of this?" Cormac held the phone closer to Dodd.

"Nothing."

"You're sure it was the same guy you saw with Tracker? One hundred percent sure?"

"Yes."

"If she's right, then it is Tracker behind all of this. How's he been pulling it off? We've been trailing him for months," Dodd said.

"Why didn't you tell me you were watching him when I told you my suspicions?"

"I thought I had ruled him out. When he had us take his little brother through, I really thought he was innocent."

"So what do you want to do?"

"He didn't leave long ago. Call the guys upstairs and put a tail on him. I want every piece of property he has watched. I want anyone he's ever spoken to in the last year watched. I want to know a complete list of the Keepers who are cooperating with him, every single last one who is involved."

Dodd pulled out his cell phone, and walked off to make the calls. I turned and watched as Cormac ran his hand along the dent on the floor, then he turned and looked to me.

"What the hell did you do? It looks like a bomb went off in here. I've never seen anything like it."

I just shrugged my shoulders. I had no clue.

Chapter Twenty-Seven

It had taken a week for the Keeper construction crew and engineers to fix the portal room, which also served as a great excuse to shut it down. Unfortunately, Tracker had fallen off the ends of the earth in that week. After he left the casino that day, he'd vanished. He wasn't answering any of Cormac's calls and there was a feeling of impending doom that hovered in the air around the penthouse. The general consensus was that he knew the curtain had been pulled back and his time was limited. Tracker's only option now was to pull out the big guns. Our problem was; we didn't know how big those guns were.

As I waited in line to order my latte that day, the very last person I expected to see was Tracker passing by the window, right on the strip, in plain sight of the casino.

"Excuse me," I said, to a woman I almost knocked over as I rushed from the coffee shop. My hand fumbled into my pocket for my phone to call Cormac while I pushed out the door to follow Tracker down the strip.

"Hello?"

"Cormac, I've got Tracker in my sights. I'm following him down the Strip."

"No. Just give me your location and wait

258

there."

"If I do that, I'll lose him."

"I don't care."

"I'm heading east down the Strip."

"Are you deaf? I said don't follow him."

"I'll call you when I get a location," I said and hung up the phone to the sound of him cursing. The ringer started chiming less than ten seconds later and I turned it off.

Why was Tracker walking? He had to be going somewhere close by, and then as if I jinxed myself, he got in a cab. I frantically waved down the next one I saw.

"Here, follow that cab, but don't let him know." I shoved two one-hundred dollar bills at him. Cormac liked all his employees to have a minimum of a thousand petty cash on them. I told him I wasn't his employee. We had compromised with the term independent contractor. He then insisted that all of his independent contractors needed to have a thousand in cash on hand at all times. I hadn't felt like arguing anymore and just took the cash. Not that it wasn't nice, I just resented his controlling nature at the time. Now I was glad. As it turned out, it wasn't such a bad policy.

"You're getting too close."

"Relax, lady, this ain't my first rodeo," the grizzled cabbie replied.

"You do this a lot?"

"You'd be amazed at the things I've done in the course of this job."

Several blocks off the strip, we slowed down around the corner from where Tracker's cab pulled up in front of a mechanic's garage.

"What are you planning to do?" the cabbie asked.

"I'm not sure. You're the one with all the experience, what would you suggest?"

He turned and looked back at me with a skeptical eye. "I'm not sure you should be going in alone. You don't look too tough."

"I'm tougher than I appear."

"If it was me, I'd get out here and circle around back."

"That's what I was thinking, too. Thanks, it was a pleasure."

"Good luck."

As I stepped out of the cab, I text messaged Cormac the location, then shut it off again. The last thing I needed was my phone giving me up. The houses were empty at this time of day, and the alleyway between them was a straight shot from here to the back entrance. A dog in the distance yelped once or twice, but quickly quieted down as I continued on my path.

I crouched down about twenty feet away, and I spotted a door and several windows all coated in dust and grime, which would work to my benefit. Creeping up to the window closest to me, I started to peek over the edge, hoping my blond hair wouldn't be spotted.

"Right on time." Tracker's voice was right behind me. "I smelled your scent all the way back on the Strip. It probably didn't hurt that I was expecting you."

I wanted to bang my head against the wall. How could I have been so stupid? He didn't just walk right in front of the Lacard. He knew Cormac had men searching every corner for him. It had been a set up, and I'd fallen right into it. All wasn't lost, I knew from past experience I could take him.

"What do you want?" I asked as I turned. That's when I saw two more men hanging back.

"I'm perfectly aware of your little tricks, Josephine. First, we are going for a ride. This dump was nothing but a decoy. Follow me."

"I don't think so." As much as I didn't want to let him just walk away, there was no way I was going somewhere with him willingly. There were three of them, but I still had a good shot of taking them down.

"Boys."

"Really, Tracker? Can't handle little old me yourself?" I asked as I watched Tracker's men step forward.

"I have a long memory."

As soon as one of his men got within range, I lashed out, and punched him squarely in the face, throwing all the energy I had into it. He was clearly hurt by the punch, but not as affected as he should have been. He was a Keeper. They both probably were.

"I wouldn't piss them off too badly, Josephine. I told your father you would be uninjured, but I can't make any promises if you carry on like this."

I felt like the wind had been knocked out of me, and I hadn't even been touched. The blood drained from my face, as I stood frozen. The words on the page rang in my head. The one who's sought is suddenly found, it will come time to stand their ground. My father. I'd been seeking him since the day I was born. Goosebumps broke out across my skin. Shit. Did this mean it was time for me to stand my ground? Stupid prophecy made it sound like *They* were all tough. It could have added a line or two in there with some instructions on what the hell I was supposed to do. Considering that Tracker's two thugs were ready to grab me and my skills were useless on them, it didn't really matter how I felt. It had been a long time coming, but a family reunion was about to finally take place and I would go stand my ground and probably be pulverized. I was guessing I'd be among the fallen, too. Real nice prophecy. Screwed again!

I nodded my head at Tracker in acquiescence.

"Get your hands off me, you slug," I said, as I pulled my arm out of the grasp of the man I hadn't hit. To give the guy credit, he didn't try to grab me, again.

"Where are we headed?" I asked once I saw the beautiful white stretch limo that sat waiting for us around the corner.

"The mountains," he replied as he held the door open for me.

"Don't you want your men back here to protect you?"

"I think I'll be fine, for now."

It irked me because he was right. Now that I'd taken the first steps toward discovering who my father was, I knew I wouldn't turn back. I'd see this out to the end.

"Since we have some time to kill, want to tell me what's going on?"

"I think what I have to tell you might make things not so black and white. Are you prepared for that?"

"Save the dramatics, will you?"

"Fine, cut and dry. You don't realize how easy the people on Earth have it. The living conditions on Romad, where I'm from, aren't as nice. I have kin who are suffering who don't need to. All I want is to be able to bring them over. That is all Vitor wants as well."

"Is Vitor part of this?"

"No, Vitor is too soft to do what's needed."

"Soft or moral?"

"Let me ask you a question. Is it moral to deny refuge to people who are suffering?"

"Where would it stop? Would you just bring a couple thousand over and play nice, or would you try to take everything?"

"Does your fear of a possible domination, that might never happen, justify not allowing people who are struggling, a chance?"

"It doesn't matter, it's not my choice."

"But it is, isn't it? Without you, they wouldn't have been able to keep it going as long as they have. You need to choose a side and quickly. And just a warning, if you choose the wrong side, you might not ever be leaving this mountain. Those are my people; I'm not leaving them to suffer when I have options."

"No matter whom you take out in the process?"

"Doesn't matter who or how many. Keep that in mind."

I believed him. He was a killer. Loyal, but still a killer.

The black of the interior of the mountain enveloped the limo as a steel garage door slid shut behind us. Within a few minutes, we slowed to a stop. I followed Tracker out of the limo into complete darkness. Even though I couldn't see a thing, the echo of our footsteps betrayed the enormity of the area. The air was cool, with lingering moisture that smelled a bit like a cellar.

Just as I was about to ask why we were in total darkness, the area was flooded with light. It was more immense than I imagined. It would put the Superdome to shame.

"How did you do this with nobody knowing?" As much as I didn't want to admire anything to do with him, I was in awe.

"It wasn't easy."

Tracker walked forward and I followed him, out of curiosity. His two men hung back but were never completely out of reach. When I saw two large monoliths similar to the ones in the portal room gleaming against the backdrop of the mountain wall, it became clear where we were headed. They had been camouflaged, initially, by the mountains own gleaming interior, but now that I saw them, they dominated even this massive space.

"Why are they so large?"

"It makes it easier to open a portal. They aren't really needed for someone very strong, but their presence aids in the ability. The larger they are, the more they aid." He looked to me in an appraising way. "My guess is if you were in full control of your abilities, you wouldn't need them at all."

"How do you know so much about this?"

"Unlike the Keepers, my race kept records."

"Records of someone else's secrets?"

"You think that is unusual? Come on now, Josephine. You aren't that naïve."

"What else do you know?"

"I know many things." He paused, as if he was unsure of himself. It was the first time I'd seen him show any vulnerability at all. "If we were friends, I might be willing to share."

"I don't have friends."

"Maybe we could be other things," he said in a voice just soft enough to reach me, but not his men. "Regardless of what you think, I'm not a bad person. I'm a survivor like you. Life isn't easy where I come from. Is it so wrong to take care of my people?"

As much as I wanted to scream at him and say he was wrong, I understood. I knew what it was like to have a tough life. Just because I didn't have a family, didn't mean I couldn't understand it.

"Ah, here's your father now."

I turned to see a tanned man with black hair who looked my age walk into the room. "Where?"

"Him," Tracker replied pointing at the man approaching.

"That guy is my age."

"I guess Cormac didn't explain the aging thing to you, yet."

"The aging thing?"

"You do know all the tales about Alchemists searching for the fountain of youth, correct?"

I nodded, realization hitting me.

"Like everything else, it doesn't always work consistently. Some of you age. I doubt you will though. Even being a half-breed, you're stronger than most. Do you know how old Cormac is?"

I was embarrassed to admit I had no idea, so I remained silent.

"I don't have an exact age, but we've got him at over two hundred."

"And how do I know you aren't a complete liar?"

"Don't you know?"

Unfortunately I did. He was telling me the truth.

"It's not an uncanny ability you have. That's a little of the Fae in you."

"Doesn't the Alchemist gene counteract the Fae?"

"Usually, but not always. There have been a few cases like yours, where instead of canceling out the other, it amplifies it."

"So, I guess you have my mother hidden somewhere in here too?"

"No, can't help you there. I have no idea where she is, neither does Hammond."

"Hammond?"

"Yes, your father."

And the surprises just kept coming.

As Hammond neared the final few steps and closed the distance between us, we eyed each other up. He was dark, surprisingly so, with black hair, tan skin, and near black eyes. I wondered if he was truly my father. Tracker believed he was, but I had my doubts.

"Hello." He spoke first. He voice was deep and gravelly and his teeth were brilliantly white against his tan skin as he gave me a hesitant smile.

"You are Hammond?"

"Yes. I'm sure you have some questions."

"I do. Why do you think you are my father?"

"You're certainly not shy. Cormac had tests run on you a while back. When you started to create a problem for Tracker, he managed to get a sample and asked me to look at them. As soon as I saw, I knew."

"And that's all you needed? Just to look at my blood?"

"I'll show you." He pulled out a knife and made a slice across his skin, light enough for just the smallest sliver of blood to pool to the surface.

My fingers tingled immediately, wanting to reach toward it. My arm acted on its own before I realized what I was doing. I caught myself and dropped it back to my side quickly.

"No, go ahead."

Too curious not to, I raised my hand back toward it, and the small stream of blood lifted and the few drops flew to my fingers.

"Neat, right?"

It wasn't exactly the term I would have used, freaky was more like it. The drops tingled on my skin.

"Here," he said as he handed me a handkerchief he had withdrawn from the inside pocket of his suit. I had a feeling he didn't use a handkerchief to appear old school, he was old school.

"Tracker said you don't know where my mother is?"

"No, I'm sorry to tell you this, but I believe she's dead."

"Why?"

"Because Malora loved me. I loved her as well. She wouldn't have disappeared like this for years if she was alive. I looked for her for a long time before I finally had to come to terms with it."

"And me?"

"I never knew you existed. I thought you died unborn with her."

"Why are you here? And with him?" I tilted my head in Tracker's direction.

"Would you walk with me?"

It wasn't exactly a walk in the park, but I followed him. He spoke once we were out of ear-

269

shot. "Tracker isn't bad."

"What he's been doing has killed people."

"Not exactly."

"I saw his brother die from radiation poisoning because of what he was doing."

"He volunteered."

"To die?" I asked, my voice laden with sarcasm.

"No, he was dying already. He only had a few months left. He offered himself up in order to help his brother, Tracker. You don't understand the existence some of them have over there. Their planet isn't anywhere near as lush as ours. I've been there. Every day is a struggle for them."

"But why do it by force? Why undermine Cormac?"

"I know Cormac better than you. When he took control, he swore to uphold the original agreement. The biggest part of that agreement is that they are only allotted a certain number of visas. One person comes, another must go.

"I understand what you are saying, I feel for his people, but this isn't the way to go about it. I don't trust him."

"I've secured your safety because you are my daughter, but that's all I can guarantee. Tracker wants you to join us. I want you to as well, but in the end, he will do what has to be done for his people. I respect that."

270

"And what about doing what is right for your people? You were Cormac's mentor, how can you go behind his back like this?"

"I'm doing what I feel is morally right."

"But, it's not. *Both* sides struck a deal. You can't decide you don't like the deal anymore, and make that choice unilaterally. What about the fact that it isn't Tracker's, Cormac's, or your choice whether to do this? How about the fact that Earth belongs to humans?"

"Hammond." Tracker's voice echoed through the cavernous area. "We are ready."

Hammond turned back to me. "I wish we could talk more, but it's time."

"Time for what?"

"To open up a new portal. Will you help?"

"You can't! If you open one up here, the whole strip could explode!"

"The other one has been shut down for a while so it's only a small likelihood."

"A small likelihood? That's okay with you?"

"We believe in our cause. Cormac is on our heels. It's now or never. It has to be done."

"No, it doesn't! You can't do this!"

"It's already in motion. The others are waiting for us to open the portal as we speak. These are good people. You'll see that it was right."

Panic seized me as I realized there was no talking him out of this, but I focused on keeping my posture as relaxed as I could. Ideas flooded through my brain but I quickly discarded them as unrealistic. I had to come up with something quick or the whole Vegas strip could be dust in minutes.

I was so distracted, I tripped on the walk back and Hammond reached a hand out to balance me. This was far from any kind of reunion I had ever imagined. I'd pictured everything from a drug dealing criminal to a drifter, but I never thought my father would want me to become a mass murderer within the first hour of meeting him.

"So?" Tracker asked, looking at both of us.

"I'm in," I said before Hammond had a chance to answer. To give him his due, his face didn't betray anything that would make Tracker think that I hadn't been on board from the get go.

"Good! The more power we can crank into this, the better," said Tracker.

"I don't have full control."

"That's okay, I'll join with you and direct your energy."

So far so good. Now I would just see if I had what it took. Sometimes in life, you have to roll a hard six.

"They are expecting us in ten minutes. Let's get this up and rolling."

A few more men entered the giant cavern and joined us as we stood around in a semicircle, and I knew if I did manage to pull this off, I wouldn't be leaving here. I wasn't sure what kind of clout Hammond had, but I doubted it would get me out of the mess I was about to make. That was, if he even bothered to try after this.

Hammond's warm hand clasped mine, and we walked forward together to stand in front of the massive monoliths.

"Are you ready?" he asked.

I wasn't, but I nodded anyway. The air in the room became charged and it tasted like I had just sucked on a penny. I felt the energy pulled through me into Hammond. As it was, the same familiar sparkling started in the center and started to grow. I didn't know how long before this wormhole would cause enough instability to set off a disturbance at the other, or how much of a disturbance, but I couldn't let it get too big or last too long.

Thinking back to what had happened in the portal room that last time, I started summoning up every horrible memory I could think of, every disastrous thing that might yet come if I couldn't stop this from happening. I had to recreate what happened the last time. I needed to make this thing implode and I knew my emotions had triggered the last time.

"What are you doing? Your energy feels erratic."

"I told you I can't control it."

"What's wrong?" Tracker asked from a few feet away.

"Nothing," said Hammond.

I continued on, thinking the worst possible thoughts imaginable. I felt Hammond's grip tighten slightly, and I saw his shoulders tense in my peripheral vision. Then he loosened his grip, trying to disengage me ever so slightly but without anyone noticing. I refused to let go. I had a death grip on his hand now, and I sensed his hesitancy.

The portal was slowly growing larger and larger, and my panic started to grow. I needed a burst of power, but I felt nothing. I was going to fail. The Lacard portal would blow up and take all those people with it. Lacey, Jonny, Buzz, Dodd, all those faces flooded through my mind. And then, I pictured Cormac's face.

Without warning, a burst of energy shot through me. Hammond gasped as it shot out of me and through him. He quickly pulled his hand from mine, but it was too late. In a split second, the wormhole filled the entire cavern, hovered at that gigantic size for a second and then imploded.

The aftershock hit us all. I barely realized what happened before I was slammed into the opposite side of the cavern and blacked out.

I woke as Cormac lifted a weight from my chest and a vibration hummed beneath me. As awareness hit me, I realized it wasn't a vibration, it was the mountain shaking.

"What's happening?"

"You tell me," he replied but didn't stop working. I looked down and realized my lower half had been completely buried in debris.

"I think I blew up the portal."

"That sounds about right. Come on." He slung my good arm around his shoulder and hoisted me up, me leaning on him as we walked out.

"Hammond is here somewhere."

"Hammond?" A flicker of emotion crossed his features and he paused for a split second, then continued on. "We don't have time. This cavern is about to collapse."

As we half jogged toward the opening I heard a moan, but I knew if he wasn't willing to stop for Hammond, he wouldn't stop for anyone.

Me in one arm, a gun in the other, he didn't rest until we got to a Range Rover he had parked about one hundred and fifty feet away. I was panting from the pain in an ankle that felt broken and was grateful to collapse onto the soft leather interior.

"Here." Cormac shoved a luke-warm water bottle at me but I was thrilled to have it. My mouth tasted like dust.

He threw the truck in gear just as I heard a loud grumbling start and I turned in time to see the top of the mountain sink into the base. The noise would've been deafening if my ears weren't already ringing.

"Is the Strip okay?"

I turned back around to see Cormac on the phone. He nodded and hung up.

"Well?"

"It's fine."

"Thank god." I closed my eyes and passed out, either from the pain or the exertion, maybe both.

Chapter Twenty-Eight

"She's still sleeping? It's been, like, twenty hours." I heard Dodd's voice from the other room as I slowly opened my eyes.

"However she did what she did, it knocked her out. She fell asleep before we even got back here," Cormac replied.

"Holy shit, are you sure she did that? That had to be some massive power," Buzz chimed in.

"It's pretty boggling, but yeah. Hammond was strong, but I've never seen anyone with that kind of energy. Even when I found her passed out in the mountain, she was still throwing off energy like I'd never felt."

I swung my legs over the edge of the bed, pushed the hair from my eyes, and stumbled toward the living room. Every part of me felt sore.

"What's going on?" I asked as I saw the three of them seated on the couches.

"You tell us," Dodd said.

"Wish I could." I plopped down on the empty seat next to Cormac, and looked to him. "What have I missed?"

"My contacts said they were going to make an announcement on the news today about what happened. People are going crazy thinking the mountain just exploded for no reason. Some are

277

saying it was aliens."

"What are they going to say?"

"Some bunk about a buildup of natural gas or something."

"Do they know what it really was?"

"No, but they are investigating it from what I heard."

"Buzz and I have to go handle a couple of loose ends. Let me know what they say."

"Don't forget to take care of Murrey," Cormac shouted after them as they were walking out of the room.

"You got it," Dodd hollered back.

"Who's Murrey?"

"Murrey's the cab driver who called to let me know Tracker took you to the mountains."

I let that little nugget digest for a moment, pondering the implications. "How many people do you have on the payroll?"

"Do you want to know just the cabbies? I could probably get that number together fairly quickly, but if you're asking for a total count, it's gonna be rough."

"Is that how you found me at the bus terminal?"

"One of the ways."

I decided not to pursue that line of questioning anymore. I decided I'd be better off in ignorance, rather than looking over my shoulder for the rest of my life.

"You said Hammond was there?"

I watched his face for the emotion I knew he must have been feeling, but he didn't let it show. "Yes. He had some interesting information."

"What did he have to say?"

"He said he was my father."

"Did you believe him?"

"I did. He did a weird blood thing, and even though I didn't understand it, I believed it. He said my mother was a woman named Malora."

"His blood came to you?"

"Yes, I guess you could say that."

"It's not a trick. You're his daughter. You know, he's tough. He might be alive. Do you want me to go back and look for him?"

I knew the offer was only for me. If it hadn't been, he would've already gone back. I understood betrayal. I didn't fault him for not going before now. "The place is crawling with people. You couldn't go back now, anyway. If he's there, they'll find him." I leaned my head against the back of the couch as I looked at Cormac. "He was willing to help Tracker even though it could kill thousands of people. That doesn't sit well with me at all, but I would've liked an opportunity to have talked to him."

"I'm telling you, he's tough. We've got a couple of days before the heat will cool down on the area, but if you want, I will go back."

I nodded, not saying anything. I didn't know what to say.

"We are pretty sure Tracker is dead."

"How sure?"

"Someone else has already taken up his position."

"They work quickly, huh?"

"Yes. Tried the portal this morning. It's already running smoothly again."

There was a heavy pause. We both knew what that meant. With the portal operating and Tracker dead, I didn't need to stay, anymore. They didn't need me, anymore; that eliminated all threats. A heavy weight settled on my chest.

"So what are your plans? Med school?"

"You know, for so long I thought that was what I wanted to do. But now, I'm not sure. I think my need to understand what I am might have been the largest draw. Now that I know, I might take a different path, I think."

"Whatever you decide to do, I can let you know when I find something out about your mother. Just let me know where you plan to be."

I smiled as I looked at him. "Do I really need to tell you?"

"No, but I didn't want to freak you out too badly."

We fell into a dead silence, just the

background noise from the TV filling the void. I looked around the room, taking in all the details that had been there for weeks but now had some strange importance to me. From the bottles that lined the bar against the wall, to the man who sat next to me. After a minute too long, I pulled my eyes from him, turning toward the distracting geologist who was speaking on the TV.

"Who is that guy?"

"Who?"

"The grey haired guy to the left of the geologist?"

"It's Senator Core. You don't recognize your own senator? Jo, you really should look at the news once in a while."

"That's the man I killed!"

"Not possible."

I turned to stare him straight in the face and grabbed the front of his shirt to emphasize how serious I was.

"That's him. Unless he has a twin, Senator Core is involved in all this."

"That, I didn't see coming."

We both stared at the TV now as the Senator took the podium and I heard that familiar voice speaking.

"This isn't good, Jo."

"No, it's not. And the guy knows exactly what I look like, too. I've got to show you something. I'll be right back." I ran into my room and grabbed the page I'd gotten from the priest.

"Where did this come from?" Cormac asked as I handed it to him.

"It was left with me when I was abandoned." I watched Cormac scan the page quickly and then turn it over and inspect the sheet itself, before scanning the words again.

"This is about you, the golden child. I'm the giver of eternal lilies."

"I know."

"Why didn't you show this to me?"

"I didn't really believe it until yesterday."

"This was ripped from a book, and I think I might know what one. It's only a legend, but then again, almost all of our history is. If I'm right, this comes from the Book of Omens."

"That does not sound good."

"It dates back to Richard. He was one of the original ten alchemists. When they were changed, Richard claimed to have visions. It was said he wrote everything down in this book."

"'Tis not the end but the start of it all.' I repeated from memory. That doesn't sound good."

"I don't think you should leave. At least not until we get a handle on how deeply this runs."

"Agreed." And strangely, I felt better.